PUTTING IT RIGHT

Nobody will ever touch my heart
the way you did
Love always
X

16-12-2005

Printed in Victoria, BC, Canada

Note for Librarians: a cataloguing record for this book that includes Dewey Decimal Classification and US Library of Congress numbers is available from the Library and Archives of Canada. The complete cataloguing record can be obtained from their online database at:
www.collectionscanada.ca/amicus/index-e.html
ISBN 1-4120-2931-7

TRAFFORD

This book was published *on-demand* in cooperation with Trafford Publishing. On-demand publishing is a unique process and service of making a book available for retail sale to the public taking advantage of on-demand manufacturing and Internet marketing. On-demand publishing includes promotions, retail sales, manufacturing, order fulfilment, accounting and collecting royalties on behalf of the author.

Offices in Canada, USA, UK, Ireland, and Spain
book sales for North America and international:
Trafford Publishing, 6E–2333 Government St.
Victoria, BC V8T 4P4 CANADA
phone 250 383 6864   toll-free 1 888 232 4444
fax 250 383 6804   email to orders@trafford.com
book sales in Europe:
Trafford Publishing (UK) Ltd., Enterprise House, Wistaston Road Business Centre
Crewe, Cheshire CW2 7RP UNITED KINGDOM
phone 01270 251 396   local rate 0845 230 9601
facsimile 01270 254 983   orders.uk@trafford.com
order online at:
www.trafford.com/robots/04-0759.html

10   9   8   7   6   5   4   3   2

PUTTING IT RIGHT

CHAPTER ONE

It was six thirty in the evening when Tom knocked on my front door. He had arrived with a few of his mates with the intention of taking me out to celebrate my sixteenth birthday. I was keen to go even though they didn't treat me particularly well, I was always the butt of their jokes, the runt of the litter was my description of myself, someone had to be although I often wondered if anyone had the misfortune of taking my place when I wasn't with them.

Tom's reputation and the fact that my father didn't like him concerned me and I had made my feelings clear earlier in the day that I didn't want him to come calling for me, trouble was Tom being Tom he just couldn't resist and he had to make his presence known, anything for the sake of confrontation. He knocked louder than he necessarily needed to and when Dad opened the door I could hear the start of an argument from where I was in my bedroom.

Dad thought Tom was a bad lot and I knew he was right but being an only child I felt I didn't have much choice other than to hang around with him and his friends as they were the only ones on the estate where I lived that were my age, surely Dad couldn't expect me to spend night after night on my own.

The commotion downstairs continued and I shrugged my shoulders at Tom's arrogance and ignorance in not respecting my request to stay away. I couldn't imagine what they were saying to each other and tried hard to block out the noise.

I pulled back the curtains a couple of inches and looking out through the window I could just make out a group of six or seven figures at the end of the garden path. My heart missed a beat as I recognised one of them. Alice. She was stunning. An on off girlfriend of Toms she always showed a little sympathy towards me over the way he and the others treated me. I was in love with her. She deserved better than Tom.

The sound behind me distracted me from what I was doing and I faced back towards the door as my father came into my room.

" They're here," he said quite sternly although I detected certain sadness in his voice, " don't expect me to bail you out."

I tried to hide my smile as he spoke but he saw me mimicking his words under my breath.

" O.K. so maybe I'm a little predictable, I just don't want you getting hurt." he said, putting a protective arm around me as I made to leave the bedroom.

" It's alright Dad," I replied, trying to release myself from his grip, " I'm sixteen today and this is one day that they won't get me down."

" Take care anyway." he instructed bending down to kiss me on the forehead. I felt a little embarrassed at his show of affection but realised it was his way of showing me how much he cared and for a brief moment I contemplated staying in. However the thought quickly disappeared as I hurried downstairs shouting goodbye in the direction of my mother before slamming the front door behind me.

Tom was facing up the garden path sharing a joke with the others as I bounded out of the house. I ran straight into him.

" You fucking idiot!" he yelled, turning around and looking angrily to where I had fallen.

" Leave it Tom."

A softer voice joined in and I looked towards the gate. It was Alice and she was walking down the path towards us. Tom continued to direct obscenities at me as he brushed away his imaginary pain.

" Shut up Tom, he didn't mean it."

The gentle voice of Alice was pleasure to my ears as she offered her hand to me to pull me back to my feet. I felt a warmness glow throughout my body as our hands touched. I looked into her blue eyes and imagined being alone with her touching more than just her hand but there wasn't much chance of that I thought as she hauled me upwards smiling at me as she wished me a happy birthday.

" Thanks." My response was mumbled as I got another warm feeling although this was more to do with shy embarrassment than my previous lust.

" Right let's go!"

I heard Toms voice and saw that he was already through the gate and walking off down the road with the others so Alice and I had to run quickly to catch up with them. As soon as we were out of sight of my house Tom reached inside his jacket pocket and pulled out a hip flask.

" Take a swig of this birthday boy!" he laughed shoving the flask towards my lips after unscrewing the cap. I didn't dare say no and took a huge gulp. I had drunk before but the burning liquid took me by surprise as it traced its route down my throat until I choked.

" What's that?" I finally spluttered, my eyes watering profusely.

" A man's drink for a little boy." Tom laughed, his glee all too obvious, as he took great delight in the way I had reacted to the fiery water and soon everybody was laughing at me, but that was nothing new. After a couple of minutes Tom regained enough composure to continue.

" It's my old mans whisky," he said before adding, " to prepare you for the night ahead."
He pushed the flask to my mouth again, this time forcing my head back and pouring in the fluid himself. Not wanting to look stupid again I swallowed hard, not allowing the whisky to beat me. Tom released his grip and looked me directly in the eyes; he seemed for a brief moment strangely pleased.

" Well done little boy," he shouted loudly at me, " tonight you will become a man."
They all ran off down the road leaving me behind wondering what he meant. I heard them launch

into a chorus of ' Happy Birthday to You.' each of them changing the words to take the piss out of me. I could take that; after all it was only words. I found myself wishing I could be as boisterous as they were but even though I'd tried to join in before I always felt so stupid. It just didn't feel right to me.

The group stopped about fifty yards ahead of me and I could see they were all holding bottles and flasks like the one Tom had. I guessed they all contained some sort of alcohol. Maybe if I drank some more then I could loosen up a little, get them to laugh with me rather than at me. I broke into a run to catch up but almost immediately began to feel self-conscious and slowed into a walk.

" Come on!" one of them shouted towards me, "or we'll be late."

" Shut up!" Tom shouted at whoever it was that had called out, " he doesn't need to know...and that goes for all of you."

I couldn't help but hear the way he spoke, he was very annoyed. I knew something wasn't quite right and I tried to find out what it was

" What's up?" I asked when I caught up with them all.

" Nothing, come join the party."

Even though it was Alice who answered my

question I wasn't convinced by her effort to reassure me. We made our way into the local playground and for a moment everything seemed to return to normal. It was a place where we as a group almost always seemed to hang around in the evenings and nothing too bad had ever happened before. I felt relieved, and even more so when each of them offered their respective bottles and flasks to me amongst mutterings of 'happy birthday'

Time went by and the banter and laughter increased, I hadn't any idea what I was drinking but I felt good. The alcohol was taking effect, I wasn't a drinker by any stretch of the imagination and it was probably affecting me more than the others. My father would definitely not approve. He was not a lover of drinking or drinkers for that matter and we never had any in the house. I looked at my watch, it was almost eight o'clock, their parents were probably in or on their way to the pub, The George, opposite to where we were now. They couldn't see us though, thanks to the hedge around the entrance, but they almost certainly knew we were there.

I glanced around the group; Alice and Tom were sat on the swings about fifteen feet from the roundabout that I was perched on. My eyes were drawn to Alice and I looked her up and down taking in her beauty. She was holding hands with Tom so I presumed that her relationship with him was back on. Still, that didn't stop me looking, and look I did, I couldn't help it. She was wearing a tight, low-cut t-shirt the thin material stretching across her developing breasts. Tom looked towards me and I quickly averted my gaze to look downwards at the ground. I didn't want to be caught staring by him but I needed another peek. Slowly I raised my eyes, drawn by the movement of the swings in front of me. I was teasing myself with my imagination and I felt a surge of warmth in my groin. My heartbeat was quickening and I thought that it would soon be so loud that everyone would be able to hear. Still I looked, her legs, covered by the knee length boots she wore, were slightly apart. Her short skirt had risen up because of the way she had sat on the wooden seat of the swing, the upward movement of which meant I could see right between her legs. How I longed to be there. Her forward thrusts through the air were coinciding with the forward thrusts in my mind. I was with her and I shut my eyes to enjoy the moment but it only meant I didn't see the nod of the head that Tom gave to one of the others. Suddenly I was spinning around on the roundabout, I wasn't holding on and I came flying out, crashing to the ground. I was pounced on by someone, my arms tightly clasped behind my back. I felt them being tied together and was aware of something being pulled around my eyes, a mask or a blindfold, whatever it was I couldn't see.

" What are you doing? Leave me alone!"
There was panic in my voice, this was something new to me, I hadn't been in a situation like this before. No one answered, whoever had been tying me up let go. I was on my knees on the ground, hands tied behind my back; my forehead was barely an inch from the grass. My pulse was racing; a million different thoughts were rushing through my head. I felt I was going to be sick and I urged once or twice. Moments passed, it felt like hours. My breathing began to settle. I couldn't see so I knew I had to calm myself down and use my ears to try and work out what was going to happen next. I held my breath and waited. It was too quiet, I felt as though I was alone.

" Hello." I ventured, nervously lifting my head half expecting a punch at any moment, but, I reasoned, they had never hit me before so why should now be any different. The thought made me feel a lot better and I moved my head around as if looking for someone to set me free.

" O.K, joke's over." I spoke confidently, surprising myself considering how terrified I had been a short time ago.

Still no one answered. I laughed inwardly; very funny I thought, tied up and left alone for God knows how long. I sighed, birthdays just don't get any better than this.

Sighing again I settled down for a long wait until they returned and released me. I made up my mind to treat it as a huge joke although it wasn't truly how I felt. I started to relax further still and pictured Alice sitting on the swing. I smiled at the image and guessed that she knew what was going to happen to me. She must have been in on the joke or she would have stopped it, she always intervened when things had seemed to be getting too far out of hand. I took it as a sign that deep down she loved me too. I smiled again.

" I love you Alice." I whispered. I wanted to shout it aloud to anyone who would listen but I couldn't, I had to keep it to myself.

Without warning I felt hands grab at the shoulders of my jacket and I was dragged to my feet. They were back. Maybe they hadn't even gone away. I was aware of voices in front of me, whoever had pulled me to my feet was still holding me by my shoulders. I imagined that I looked like a prisoner facing a firing squad. Any last requests? Yes to screw Alice in front of you, you bastard. I gave Tom an icy stare, I felt I could,

I was wearing a blindfold.

" Quiet!"

The voice of Tom rang out and the background chatter of the others ceased as they listened to what he had to say.

" I'm sorry," he began, directing his apology at me but I didn't believe his sincerity, " I'm sorry we've had to tie you up but we have a little surprise for you and it's time to go and get it."

I heard giggles from the others, I wasn't quite sure if Alice was joining in. I listened, assuming that if she was laughing then things weren't going to be too bad.

" Quiet!" Tom announced again, " it's time for Rufus Reynolds to become a man."

The grip on my shoulders relaxed and I thought I would be finally free of my bonds but instead I felt myself being pushed forwards. Without the use of my arms for balance I almost fell, but someone was in front of me and held me upright. Their hands were softer. It was Alice. I felt her breath on my face as our cheeks momentarily touched. I wanted to kiss her. One day I told myself, one day. More choruses of 'Happy Birthday' rang out as we made our way out of the playground. I heard the sound of the piano playing in the George as we passed but I soon lost my bearings. I didn't know where I was. The singing continued and the laughter increased but so did the pushes in the back and the digs in the ribs. I stumbled many times. Every so often a bottle was forced between my lips and I had no choice but to drink. I think I was drunk and my mood was changing with every step. I tried talking to them but no one was listening, not even Alice.

" Fuck you!" I kept repeating, even directing one at Alice, I regretted it almost immediately but still the thought was of why wouldn't she help me, couldn't she see how scared I was?

Finally I got the impression we had arrived at our destination, we were in a field of some description but where it was I wasn't sure. The pushing had stopped and all I wanted was to be free.

" Can't you take this fucking blindfold off?" I shouted angrily.

" Not until you've had your present." Tom replied.

Another push in the back and we were walking again, the feeling under my feet had changed and we were on some sort of stony path. I heard a creak as if a huge door was opening and felt a change in temperature as I was led into some sort of building. A familiar smell filled my nostrils and I realised we were in a farmyard barn. I was confused, what sort of present would be waiting for me here. I was pushed to the ground but the landing was soft and it took a matter of seconds to take in that we were in a hay barn. I was hoping that my hands would be untied and the blindfold removed but instead I felt hands grabbing at the button and zip of my trousers and they were yanked down forcibly, quickly followed by my pants. My jacket and t-shirt were pulled up to my chest to leave me lying there on full view to everyone. I tried to turn over to hide myself but was in such a position that it was impossible. I heard the comments they were making and tried to block them out as best I could.

" Ssshhhush," Toms voice broke through the noise and the laughter stopped.

" Roo," he said to me softly, " it's your sixteenth birthday today and this is our present to you."

I was listening intently to him desperate for a clue as to what was going to happen next. I had an awful feeling they were either going to shave my groin or paint my private parts some strange colour.

" There comes a time," Tom continued, " when a boy has to become a man. Our way of saying sorry to you for the past few years of torment is to rid you of your innocence. After tonight you will no longer be a virgin."

I couldn't believe what I was hearing, I was expecting something a lot more derisive but it was nothing to what I heard next.

" Alice." he commanded, and I felt a hand take hold of my penis. It couldn't be could it? All my dreams come true. Not here surely, not in front of everyone. I felt all my blood rushing to where I was being touched, the warmness racing through every vein as the hand gently caressed my manhood.

" Alice." I heard myself murmur and I swallowed hard. My penis grew faster than it ever did in the privacy of my bedroom, this was so different, this was real. I wanted to reach out and touch her as well but I couldn't I was too tightly restrained. I heard her voice as she excitedly encouraged me, massaging me to my fullness.

" Are you ready?" Alice whispered in my ear.

" Yes, I want you now." My eagerness sounded like I was begging but I didn't care, this was the best moment of my life. Where I was didn't matter any more, all I wanted was to be joined with Alice. I felt her body climb on top of me guiding my stiffness towards her and I almost came the moment our intimate places touched. I entered her quickly and easily and she began moving up and down my length, slowly at first but getting faster. I wanted her to take her time as much as I wanted it to reach its goal.

" Yes," she was shouting, " fuck me Roo."

PUTTING IT RIGHT

I was nearly done, I couldn't hold back any longer, I wished I could see her face and it was as if wishes were made to come true. My blindfold was ripped from my eyes just at the moment I exploded into her. I looked into her eyes, arching into thrusting spasms as I emptied my body into hers, only it wasn't Alice.

CHAPTER TWO

It seemed an eternity before they released me from the horrific vision I had just encountered, finally cutting the rope from around my wrists and sending me on my way. I heard Alice and Tom arguing as I ran from the barn and could vaguely recollect her fists pummelling his chest. I couldn't see too much because of the tears that were pouring down my face. Stupidly I hoped that maybe this was for the best and it would somehow split them up for good. What was I thinking? This had just turned from something pleasurable into the worst experience of my life and Alice had been a part of it. How could she whisper those things in my ear knowing all the time I wasn't even fucking her.

" Bitch." I yelled struggling with the button of my trousers as I raced down the gravel track that led to the barn.

" Fucking bastards."

I was beginning to get hysterical and I was running too fast, I tripped over my feet and fell headlong into the ground. My hands weren't quick enough to stop my fall so my head hit the ground hard. I slid forwards, the stones of the track biting into the flesh of my face. I felt the warm sensation of blood mingling with my salty tears and it began to sting. I was crying uncontrollably.

CHAPTER THREE

I was aware of something tapping me on my head and across my back. With a great deal of pain I managed to turn my head to look upwards. I felt the cold drips of rain against my skin and it was strangely refreshing. I gingerly turned over onto my back to face the night sky to get the benefit of something that felt so good. The drops started getting heavier, increasing all the time until I realised it was pouring. I jumped to my feet and looked around for somewhere to take shelter. I glimpsed the barn and suddenly everything came rushing back to me.

I looked at my watch; it was twenty past one in the morning. I must have passed out; surely it couldn't have been that late. I looked at the barn. They wouldn't still be in there, they would have gone home by now. They would have just left me where I was without a second thought. I remembered they had shut me in a cupboard at school when I was just ten years old and forgot about me. Six hours I had been left there before the caretaker found me. I'd cried for a while and then just fallen asleep. A bit like tonight, I reasoned. No nothing like tonight, I remonstrated with myself as images from earlier spread through my mind.

Convinced that nobody was around I made my way back to the barn, stepping through the puddles that were forming on the uneven track. I paused at the entrance to listen just in case. Satisfied that I was alone I went inside to shelter. As soon as I was undercover I turned to face outside, I didn't want any visual reminders of what had happened. I shivered; I was cold from the soaking I had just had. I needed to think. I leant on the frame of the doorway and stared into the blackness of the night.

I wondered where I was and how I was going to get home. That's when it hit me a little harder, the thoughts of home and my parents. What were they going to say, I must look a right state. I started to get a little agitated, I needed to clean myself up, I couldn't let them see me like this. I went back outside and turned my face skywards, raising my hands to brush the falling water about my broken skin. It stung for a while but it had to be done.

Satisfied I had removed most of the blood and grime from my face I stepped back inside and reached into my trouser pocket to pull out a handkerchief. I held it to my face to dry away the water and any blood that was still seeping from my injuries. After a minute I took the cloth away and looked at it. A few traces of blood were visible and I was slightly relieved that it didn't appear too serious. I decided I would tell my parents that I had fallen from the roundabout, it wasn't a lie it just wasn't what had caused the damage to my face. Why was I late home? I'd had a bit too much to drink so I needed to sober up and it had taken much longer than I had hoped. Feeling pleased with the excuses I'd come up with I looked outside again. The rain was easing. It was time to make my way home. The rain could add to my excuses because it would easily explain my dishevelled appearance. I made my way outside; I had a vague idea where I was. I was sure the farm was somewhere we had been before. I guessed we had walked for about two miles, the same sort of distance as when we had set fire to a few stacks of hay last summer. It had been Tom's idea, it always was, I had tried to get out of it but was dragged along anyway. I thought it was just a show of Tom's bravado and I was really shocked when he actually flicked the match at the piles of hay. I don't think I have ever run as fast to get away from anything as I did that night. We hid in a wooded area close to the farm and waited as the fire brigade came and dealt with the blaze. I was terrified that we were going to get caught but we weren't, we stayed until all the commotion had died down and then sneaked home. It was everything that Dad had warned me about and I felt sure that I was on my way to jail. I kept my distance from Tom for weeks after that but then gradually I started to hang around with him and his mates again.

If it was the same farm then I knew that if I kept to the track I would reach the road that led back to town.

The rain had virtually stopped as I headed off down the track and the clouds were moving quickly across the night sky. The moon was putting in an appearance and the light from it helped my eyes adjust to the darkness. I followed the track for about five hundred yards and my feet were soaking from stepping in too many unseen puddles. Eventually I spied the gate set back about fifty feet from the road. Wearily I climbed it and jumped down on the other side. I ran the last few yards and stopped when I reached the welcoming surface of the road. I looked both ways and began to grin. I was right, getting home was going to be easy now.

It took almost an hour to reach my house, I had hurried to begin with but my feet hurt so much I had to slow down. I'd spent every second of that hour going over and over in my mind the horror of what I had been through. How could anyone be so sick as to even think of doing such a thing to anybody. I'd cried much of the way back, I didn't think I would ever be able to stop but the nearer I got to home the more determined I was to stop the flow of tears.

I reached the end of my road and looked towards my house, checking to see if any lights were on. I hoped not, I couldn't bear to face my parents at that moment. I glanced at my wrist to find out the time, it was nearly three. I'd been late before and my parents hadn't waited up, but never this late. I wasn't even sure if I had ever been awake at this hour. I could see the hallway light on as I neared the garden gate but the front room light was off. This was a good sign, if they were waiting up for me then all the lights would have been on.

I walked up the path as quietly as I could, putting my hand in my pocket as I went. I fumbled around for a few seconds before pulling out the object I was seeking. I held the key between my thumb and forefinger and for a moment just stared at it. My heart started beating a little quicker as I reached out to place the key into the lock. I felt so nervous I was shaking but finally I managed to push the key into the hole. As slowly as possible I turned it not wishing to make a sound, and as the lock clicked I pushed gently on the door. It swung open more easily than I expected and I had to reach out quickly to hold it still before it slammed into the wall. I paused momentarily before entering the house checking that all was quiet, it was, all I had to do now was climb the stairs and get into the safety of my bedroom.

Carefully I closed the front door behind me and tiptoed across the hallway to the bottom of the stairs. I looked up and listened, still not a sound. A couple of times the stairs creaked under my weight as I made my way up them and I hesitated, terrified that I would disturb my sleeping parents. I reached the landing at the top; it wasn't far to go now. My bedroom was at the far end, past my parents' room, the bathroom and the toilet. Walking past the first door seemed to take forever but once I'd made it my pace quickened and within seconds I was shutting my bedroom door behind me.

The relief on reaching my sanctuary was instant; I began to fall to pieces. The tears flooded my face like a tidal wave and I screwed up my eyes to try and stem the flow. It was no use, I had to let go. I began ripping my clothes off until I stood naked. I was shaking, my fists clenched tightly by my sides, my teeth clamped together so forcefully I thought they would shatter. I felt the anger welling up fiercely inside. I needed to hit out at something and I did, myself, as if somehow I could beat away the pain. I punched myself hard in the stomach, the chest and the groin. I grabbed my penis and tried to rip the filthy organ from my body. I didn't want it any more; if I could just get rid of it then I would be a virgin again. I screamed inwardly but how I longed to scream out loud. I let go of my penis and looked at my hands. I stared at them, eyes wide and wild. It was impossible but I knew it was there, the filth, the dirt and the smell of the insides of another man. I flung myself onto my bed, the softness of which should have been a comfort to me but I didn't notice. I grabbed hold of the pillow and wrapped it around my head, I was sobbing uncontrollably and I needed something to try and mask the sound. I think I cried all night.

CHAPTER FOUR

I was awakened by the sound of the milk float at about six thirty in the morning. The clattering of the glass outside my window as the milkman sorted out how many bottles he was going to leave us stirred me from my slumber. My eyes felt red raw and I couldn't imagine what I looked like. I was cold and realised I was still lying naked on top of my bed covers. I shivered and climbed inside. It was warm from where I had been lying and I felt glad. I pulled the sheet and blanket over myself and tugged the pillow down behind my head. I felt safe. My mind began to remember the night before and tears began to fill my eyes again. I didn't know what I was going to do. I needed a bath but I had to stay where I was until both my parents were out of the way. I couldn't let them see me at least not until I'd had the chance to clean myself up.

Dad would be off to work soon and I could hear sounds from his bedroom as he was getting ready. I imagined Mum to be downstairs preparing his breakfast or polishing his shoes. They were a happy couple, so devoted to each other and to me and I didn't want to do anything that would disrupt that harmony.

Time passed by and Dad went downstairs, I could hear muffled voices in the distance as they conversed freely in the kitchen, planning the day ahead. Moments later the front door banged shut and Dad was off to work. One down and one to go. My thoughts were cruel, I mused, but justified considering the physical and mental state I was in. I started to yawn, my eyelids were getting heavy, it was only seven thirty and Mum wouldn't be going anywhere for hours. I was tired and wanted to go back to sleep. I pulled the covers tighter around my body and closed my eyes. I tried to imagine the happier times of my life but the horror of the previous night seemed to be permanently etched in my mind. The vile image of when the blindfold was ripped from me played over and over again. Eventually my exhausted body could take no more and I drifted away from my torment to the comparative safety of sleep.

It was five hours later that I re-awoke and I felt almost refreshed. I listened for sounds in the house but I couldn't hear any. I lifted my head from the pillow and leant on my elbows. I could see my bedroom door and it was slightly ajar. I was pretty sure that I had closed it when I got home so I guessed that my mother must have come in to see me and then gone again without shutting the door behind her. Suddenly it didn't matter anymore if Mum was in the house, I could still make it to the bathroom without her seeing me if I was careful. I desperately needed to see what I looked like before I could face the rest of the day. I pushed the covers right back and forced myself out of bed. I walked towards the door and took my dressing gown down from the peg it was hanging on. I put it on, tying the cord around my waist, and then opening the door a little bit further, I peered out. I could see that the bathroom door was wide open which I assumed meant no one was in there. I moved quickly across the landing and once inside closed the bathroom door behind me, not forgetting to slide the bolt into place so that I wouldn't be disturbed. Next I turned to face the mirror on the wall and braced myself for a shock. What a mess, the blood that I thought I'd managed to wash off in the rain was spread all over my face. I looked like I'd been in a boxing match and the wounds appeared to be much more serious than I had thought.

I felt a pain in my stomach and realised that I needed to relieve myself but I couldn't afford the risk of going to the toilet next door looking the way I did, there was nothing else I could do, I removed my gown and urinated in the bath. As disgusting as it seemed I had no choice. When I had finished I flushed it away until I was satisfied I'd removed all trace of it. Putting in the plug I then began to fill the bath. Steam filled the air as hot water gushed from the tap. I couldn't wait to get in and soak my weary bones. I turned off the hot water and turned on the cold, swirling the water around the bath until I'd reached what I considered to be the right temperature. Gingerly I lowered my body into the tub, the warmness enveloped me as I lay back and closed my eyes and for the first time in ages I felt completely relaxed as I drifted off into an imaginary world of make believe.

It must have been nearly an hour later when the knock at the door startled me, drawing me back into the real world.

" Are you alright in there son?" the shrill pitch of my mother's voice rang out as she posed the question.

It took me a while to adjust to the fact that I was no longer alone and my heart jumped as I struggled to find the words to answer.

" Rufus!" my mother's voice was more demanding this time.

" Yeah," I mumbled, " I'm alright, I'll be out in a minute."

The water was cold and rather than add more

warm I got out, pulling the plug as I went. Wrapping a towel around my body I moved towards the door and listened. My mother had gone back down the stairs so it was safe to return to my room. I rubbed myself down with the towel once I'd got there taking care when drying my face as one or two of the cuts were still sore. Dropping the towel in a heap on the carpet I pulled some clothes from out of my wardrobe and put them on. Once dressed I sat down on my bed and waited until I had plucked up enough courage to go downstairs.

CHAPTER FIVE

For the next two weeks I hid myself away, I knew the ridicule I faced if I made an appearance in the outside world. I had managed to explain my injuries to my parents as an accident that I had sustained in the playground but I wasn't sure if they believed me, still that was up to them, I could never tell them the truth. They knew something was wrong but I refused to talk about it and they grew increasingly concerned by my odd behaviour. They called the doctor out twice but I wouldn't see him, refusing to come out of my bedroom. I found myself yelling at them, something I had never done in my entire life.

" It's not a fucking medical problem." I snapped through gritted teeth on one occasion, reducing my poor mother to tears. I could see how much they just wanted to help but I kept on hurting them all the same.

One of the first things I did was go up into the loft when my parents were out and unpack a box of my childhood toys, teddy bears, cars, books and the like. I took great comfort from them, playing with them for hours in my bedroom. It was my way of blocking out the events of my birthday, a subconscious return to my boyhood innocence.

For the first three or four days Alice and Tom knocked on my front door. I didn't know what they were hoping to say that would make anything even remotely beneficial to me. I was generally a forgiving person but my mind was in so much turmoil how could I ever forgive them. I couldn't even comprehend how they could do such a thing in the first place.

It seemed I was crying all the time, especially at night. Everything was so lonely in the dark. I couldn't sleep; I'd lie awake for hours reliving the horror. Even when I did manage to fall asleep the dreams or rather the nightmares were always the same. I couldn't see that there would ever come a time when I would be at peace with myself.

It was after about ten days and early in the afternoon when I heard a knock on the front door. I was alone in the house, in my bedroom as usual. My father had gone to work and Mum was out somewhere. I didn't answer the door, I never did any more. The knocking continued but I wasn't going to respond to it no matter who it was. I peered through a gap in the curtains and I could just about make out who it was standing on the doorstep. It was Alice and she was alone. I looked down the path towards the gate to see if Tom was skulking around but I couldn't see anyone. It didn't make any difference if he was there or not, I still wasn't going to answer the door. I widened the gap in the curtains to about two feet, just enough to make myself visible if Alice were to look upwards. It was the first time the curtains had been open since my birthday.

Alice stopped knocking and turned to walk away up the path. It seemed like forever since I had seen her. She looked so perfect; I wished she would look up towards me so that I could see her face. I was aware of my right hand slipping down the inside of my trousers. It was a tight fit so I quickly released my button and zipper with my left. My hand continued downwards and inside my underpants. I took hold of my penis as I continued to watch Alice. It felt good, I hadn't held myself for so long I had forgotten what it felt like. I could feel myself growing between my fingers and within seconds I had reached my full size. I started to slowly caress myself as my trousers fell around my ankles, momentarily I released my grip on my penis so that I could tug my pants down to give myself more freedom.

When I looked back out of the window I saw that Alice was looking up at me. Our eyes met and she gave me a little smile. My hand clenched tight around my length as I watched her raise her hand

and point towards the door. She mouthed the word 'please' as she pointed but I shook my head to say no. I began to masturbate and I didn't stop until I had finished, staring at Alice the whole time. I fell to my knees afterwards and didn't look out of the window again until it was dark. Alice was long gone, I didn't know if she knew what I had been doing but I felt that now I was ready to speak to her.

I was downstairs in the kitchen when my mother returned home. That was unusual in itself as I'd been keeping my distance from her and my father. She saw me from the hallway and we just stood looking. I wanted to rush to her and have her hold me in her arms and she must have felt the same, we met halfway and flung our arms around each other. Tears were flowing, not only from me but from my mother as well. It was a massive relief for me; it was as though I was finally coming to terms with everything. I wanted to tell all but knew that was something for the future, now wasn't the right time, there were others I needed to talk to first.

I was still in the kitchen talking to my mother when Dad arrived home from work. I didn't hear him come into the house and I didn't notice him listening in the doorway. I was laughing at something that Mum had said when I caught sight of him out of the corner of my eye. Turning to face him I offered a little smile. It was all he needed and I swear I saw a tear fall from his eye as he looked back at me. I'd seen him cry before, at my grandmother's funeral, but this was different. There was a certain sparkle in his eyes as he too broke into a smile. I couldn't imagine how happy he was feeling inside. He came over and put his arms around me hugging me so tight that I thought he would never let me go.

We talked a lot over our evening meal, Mum and Dad kept asking awkward questions about what had happened but I told them that I wasn't ready to answer yet and I wasn't sure I ever would be. I told them all I wanted to do was to be able to forget and move on with my life. Dad began blaming Tom for everything saying I should never see him or his friends again. I couldn't disagree could I because I felt the same although once I ventured outside I knew that I would bump into him sooner or later. Alice was different; I wanted to bump into her. I asked Mum and Dad that if she ever came calling again to invite her indoors so that I could talk with her. Although they promised they would, I was still left with the impression that they would turn her away. Secretly I hoped that she would call when they were both out.

We relaxed together in the front room in the evening after we had tidied up from the evening meal. No one said a word, we were just content with each other's company. As was always the case in the early part of the evening it wasn't long before they were both dozing. I disappeared upstairs and lay on my bed thinking. I'd had a good day but it was just one day. I still had a long way to go.

CHAPTER SIX

The days passed by quite quickly and I was becoming more like my old self, although for now it was just in the company of my parents as I still didn't feel brave enough to go out. Alice hadn't been back and I was beginning to think that I had made a mistake in not talking to her the last time she came around. She was constantly on my mind and as I was still spending the majority of my time in my bedroom I always seemed to be gazing out of the window hoping to catch a glimpse of her. I'd stopped playing with my old toys but I wouldn't put them back in the loft just in case I had a bad day and needed things to occupy my mind. I'd pushed most of them under my bed but I still kept one or two of my teddy bears tucked under my blankets. I wasn't ready to relinquish the comfort they brought to me at night no matter how sane I was during the day.

It was raining steadily the day I finally spotted Alice walking on the opposite side of the road to our house. My window had steamed up where I had been gazing through the glass and I quickly rubbed away the moisture. I waved excitedly at her but she didn't seem to notice. I wasn't sure if she had even looked across towards me. I was only wearing a pair of shorts and a vest but I ran downstairs and flung open the front door.

" Alice." I shouted, running down the path.

She had gone past my house and was continuing on her way up the road.

" Alice." I shouted again, this time a little louder.

She turned her head to look at me but didn't stop walking. It didn't occur to me that this was the first time I'd been outside my front gate as I ran up the road towards her. I was soaking wet by the time I reached her but I didn't care, I needed to do it.

" Alice," I panted, almost out of breath, " wait please, I want to talk."

" I can't," she responded, " I've got to meet Tom."

She continued on her way almost pushing right through me. It wasn't quite the reaction I was looking for and ashamedly I grabbed her shoulder bringing her to a halt.

" Fuck Tom!" I shouted angrily, " what about me?"

I looked into her eyes and saw her discomfort and I immediately regretted being so rough with her.

" I'm sorry," I said softly, releasing my grip on

her shoulder, " but I need to know why? You owe me an explanation."

" Not now," she started, taking a step backwards as if to get away from me, " I mean, I can't right now. I really do have to meet Tom."

" When then?" I interrupted; I was beginning to feel a little hurt by her attitude.

" I don't know, how about tomorrow?"
I looked at her for a few seconds hoping to catch a flicker of honesty in her eyes but she turned her head away from me.

" Do you promise?" I said as sadly as I could in a selfish effort to play on her emotions.

" Yes, I promise." Alice replied and for the first time she looked me directly in the eyes. I felt as though she meant what she was saying.

" I really do have to go." Alice continued and unexpectedly touched me on the arm. See, I told myself, she does care.
I stood on the pavement and watched her hurry away up the road until she disappeared from view.

" Bye." I mumbled when I could no longer see her. Sighing deeply I turned around and slowly made my way back home.
It was only when I got back inside that I was aware of how soaking wet I was and I quickly went upstairs to the bathroom to remove my sodden clothes. I flung them on the floor,

promising myself I would pick them up before my parents came back home. I dried myself off with the towel that was hanging over the edge of the bath and when I had finished I threw it to join the wet pile of clothes on the floor. I shivered as I made my way across the landing to my bedroom, where I quickly dressed.

I went towards the window and looked out, half hoping to see Alice standing outside waiting to see me. My head had started spinning, so many thoughts were rushing around and none of them were making any sense. I needed to calm down, take stock and think rationally. I wished I had agreed a definite time with Alice. I started to feel sick; maybe I wasn't as ready for it as I thought I was. I ran back towards the toilet as I felt a sudden surge from my stomach and I just managed to bend over the toilet bowl as the urge reached my throat. Thankfully nothing came out. I urged a few more times over the next ten minutes, each one a little less forceful than the one before until I finally stopped. I sat on the floor next to the toilet for ages afterwards, my stomach hurting from all the retching. I wanted a glass of water but thought I had better wait until the pain had subsided just in case I brought it back up.

I felt a bit calmer now and my thoughts turned back towards Alice. There was so much I wanted to say to her I didn't know where to begin. I needed to plan ahead. I got up from the floor and poured a glass of water from the hand basin, gulping it down confident that it would be leaving my body by its normal route.

Back in my bedroom I opened one of my cupboard drawers and pulled out a notebook and pen. I intended to write down just what I needed to ask Alice but after half an hour the only question I could come up with was simply...WHY? I tossed the book and pen onto the floor and lay back on my bed. I decided it would be better if the situation were left emotional instead of pre-planned and clinical. I closed my eyes and pictured a happy smiling Alice, I smiled too before I drifted off to sleep.

I woke an hour later feeling suitably refreshed. My stomach hurt but this time it was through hunger. I sauntered downstairs to the kitchen to make myself a sandwich. My mother was in the dining room drinking a cup of coffee when I went in. I must have slept quite heavily as I hadn't heard her return. We greeted each other cheerily.

" Sorry about the mess in the bathroom Mum," I said, " I'll clean it up later."

" What happened?" she asked, " did you get in the bath with your clothes on?"

I smiled and told her about Alice. I noticed her

frown slightly before I continued saying that Alice would be coming round sometime the next day and that I would be grateful if she could be out for the day. She wasn't too happy about it but after some persuading she finally agreed.

CHAPTER SEVEN

I didn't get much sleep that night. Every time I started to drift off another stark image from my birthday flashed into my mind. Over and over again I replayed the horror of that night. I was even beginning to feel unsure about meeting with Alice the next day. The eager anticipation I had felt a few hours earlier had been replaced by a sense of dread. I was absolutely terrified and I wished that I had drawn up that list of what to say, but it was too late. I couldn't do it at such a late hour. I tried to focus my attention on other things, even resorting to counting sheep but found it amazing that I could have so many different thoughts at exactly the same time. I desperately needed to sleep and finally, thankfully, I managed a little.

I was wide-awake before my alarm went off. I wasn't too concerned about the time until I heard the repetitive ring. I'd been lying awake for an age, hands clasped together behind my head just staring at the ceiling. I wasn't thinking of anything in particular just content with watching the room get lighter as the day began to break. I'd set the alarm for six o' clock and as it burst into life I remembered what lay ahead. I planned on getting up early, mainly because I didn't know what time Alice would arrive. I guessed that it wouldn't be before nine as she wouldn't turn up while my parents were in but I still had to be ready just in case. I flicked the switch on the clock to silence it, swinging my legs around until I was sitting on the edge of the bed. I yawned and instinctively stretched my arms outwards. I didn't feel too bad considering I hadn't slept much. I yawned again, this time rubbing my eyes before I finally made a move to get dressed. As I did so I decided to make Mum and Dad a cup of tea hoping that this would explain why I was up so early. Mum would know the truth but I'd begged her not to tell Dad, as I knew he would try and stop me from seeing Alice. I didn't like lying to anyone, especially my father, but what he didn't know couldn't hurt him.

Hurriedly I made my way to the kitchen knowing my mother would soon be up to prepare Dad's breakfast as she did so every morning. I put the kettle on to boil and the sugar and milk into the two cups that Mum had already left out the night before. Mum came into the kitchen just as the kettle boiled.

" Lord save us," I heard her say, " it's a miracle."

" Thanks Mum," I smiled, " but at least wait until you taste it!"

Mum smiled back and watched me as I poured the tea from the pot into the cups. It didn't look too bad but I didn't have a cup myself.

" Don't worry love," Mum started, kissing me on top of my head as I prepared to take Dad's tea upstairs to him, " I haven't told him."

I felt relieved and grateful that Mum had kept her promise and vowed to myself that I would do her a favour in return. I duly delivered the hot drink to Dad and we exchanged the normal morning pleasantries. I didn't want to talk too much and Dad was in a bit of a rush, so I disappeared back into my bedroom. I looked at my watch for the time, moving towards the window as I did so. It was still too early but I drew the curtains back and looked out across the front garden. No one was there. I lifted myself up and sat on the windowsill to watch, I hoped I wouldn't be waiting too long.

Half an hour later I replied to my father's shouts of goodbye and my eyes followed him as he strolled down the road towards the bus stop. I secretly envied my father; he was a proud man who loved his work no matter how poorly he was paid. He had little to show for his working life but he never complained.

I continued to stare at the outside world, watching

as more and more people began to go about their daily routine, most heading towards the bus stop to join my father as he stood waiting. Another ten minutes and it would be all quiet again before the next rush, this time of children as they made their way to school. I thought of school and realised it was somewhere I hadn't been for nearly two months. My parents and the doctor had arranged something with my headmaster to explain my absence. I didn't care what they had decided as I was leaving in less than six months time. I thought I would probably go back after Christmas but as I wasn't going to take any exams I thought it would be a complete waste of time. I didn't know what I was going to do for a job when I finally left but thought I could probably pick up an apprenticeship somewhere in town, there seemed to be plenty about. It didn't matter to me what it was because I didn't know much about anything. The only thing the teachers said I was any good at was making people laugh, and that wouldn't get me anywhere.

Time passed on and I was still sat on the ledge when Mum tapped on my bedroom door and came in.

" I'm off into town to do some shopping," she said to me, " I'll be back as late as I can."

" Thanks Mum, I really do appreciate this." I

replied trying to sound as sincere as possible.

Mum came across the room and gave me a hug, playfully tickling me under the ribs as she let go. I followed her downstairs and closed the front door behind her as she left. I looked again at my watch as I went into the front room. It was almost nine thirty; suddenly I began to feel quite nervous. I thought it best that I met with Alice in the front room and I walked around moving ornaments, straightening pictures and generally tidying up. Satisfied that everything was neat and tidy I once again looked out through the window. There was still no sign of Alice. Even though it was a school day I was sure that she would call sooner rather than later. She did have a tendency to play truant especially when she wanted to meet Tom, as she must have done yesterday when I saw her.

I settled down into the comfort of the settee and waited. I didn't have long to wait. Within five minutes there was a gentle tapping on the front door. I jumped up from where I was sat and took a peek through the curtains. Alice was stood at the door waiting for me to answer. I tripped in my rush to let her in, scraping my forearm against the sideboard as I stumbled through the lounge doorway.

" Hello Alice." I said as I opened the door before turning my attention back to my self-inflicted wound. It had started to bleed.

" Shit." I muttered to myself. This wasn't quite the greeting I had imagined. I pulled a handkerchief from my trouser pocket and pushed it against my arm. The blood seeped through staining the cloth as I held it tight.

" Can I help?" Alice inquired softly, reaching out towards me.

" No, it's nothing." I replied rather too abruptly, pulling away from her.

Alice wasn't deterred by my rudeness and she again reached out to help with my injury. This time I relented and allowed her to take control. She led me into the kitchen where she bathed my arm under the cold water before gently drying it with a clean hand towel.

" Do you have a first aid box?" she asked.

" Up there." I replied, pointing with my free arm towards the cupboard where it was kept. Alice reached up and took down the box removing the lid and taking out all that she needed to strap me up. I watched her intently as she went about her task, in awe of how grown up she seemed even though she was still only fifteen.

" There, all done." she said proudly as she clipped the safety pin together. She looked up into my eyes giving me a reassuring smile. I smiled back. I wanted to give her a kiss, but settled with offering my thanks.

" Would you like a drink?" I asked, it was my turn to try and act grown up and I went through a list of what I had to offer. She finally settled on a glass of lemonade and I poured us one each, grabbing the biscuit barrel as we made our way to the front room.

My accident and Alice's subsequent kindness had seemed to take away the nervousness I had been feeling and as we settled into the two armchairs opposite each other I blurted out the question.

" Why?"

CHAPTER EIGHT

I looked apprehensively at Alice as I waited to hear what she had to say in answer to my question. She lowered her head and peered into her lemonade. I noticed how pale her face had turned and for a moment I wished I didn't have to put her through any of what I had to ask her. Why couldn't I just forget about it? But I had to know and Alice was the only person I wanted to hear it from.

" Why Alice?"

She was taking too long to answer and my impatience got the better of me as I again posed the same question. I wasn't angry, I was pleading with her hoping to coax an answer, yet when she raised her head and looked straight at me I noticed there were tears in her eyes.

" It wasn't meant to be like that." she started to say.

" So what was it meant to be like?" I interrupted, the volume of my voice increasing as I took offence to what she was saying.

" I'm sorry." Alice's tears were really flowing now and even though I think it was the first time I had ever seen her like it, it only served to make me more determined to find out why she had done what she did.

" I need more than sorry Alice," I said firmly, " I need to understand why you of all people could do that to me."

" It was Tom's idea." she sobbed the words slowly and again I interrupted only this time sarcastically.

" I sort of guessed that."

" Please," Alice begged me, " let me finish and then you can judge me."

It was my turn to be sorry, I realised I wasn't giving her a chance and she was right I was judging her too soon, after all it was me who wanted her to explain.

" I'm sorry." I said quietly, I was determined not to interrupt again.

Alice beckoned me towards her and I moved to sit down at her feet. She reached out and took my hand in hers, she was shaking and her skin felt cold. We looked at each other for a few moments until she was ready to talk again.

" It was meant to be a birthday surprise." Alice began. I felt the urge to answer back but bit my tongue, some fucking birthday surprise I thought to myself. Alice continued to look at me and I'm sure she knew what I wanted to say as she gave my hand a reassuring squeeze. I noticed she wasn't shaking as much and she was beginning to warm up. That made me feel good and I relaxed and let her continue.

" We were going to get a girl to do it, you know, to do it with you, we wanted to give you a good time to make up for all the shit we've given you in the past."

" So what changed?" I asked, I had to say something; I wasn't expecting to hear that it had started as something innocent.

" Tom did." Alice replied and then paused as if waiting for me to say something else. Strangely I didn't feel angry any more and although I was mentally picturing 'that night' I began to feel that Alice was telling me the truth. I needed to hear more before I could answer.

" After we had made plans for you and the girl, Tom began to get resentful. He couldn't understand why we wanted to make you happy. He kept accusing me of wanting you myself. He persuaded the others to go along with his new plan one day when I wasn't around. I was so angry, we had our biggest row ever. I told him we were finished."

" So why couldn't you have warned me?" I asked, " If you were that angry you could have stopped it."

" I wanted to believe me, but he had a hold on me, I had to do what he wanted."

" That's rubbish Alice, no one can make you do something that you don't want to do."

" It's the truth, honestly, he began blackmailing me, he threatened to tell my Dad we were having sex."

" But you're going out with Thomas James, I'm sure your Dad knows he's fucking you!"

My response was cold and just a little cynical; I knew there was more to it than what Alice was telling me.

" Maybe," she replied, " but Tom had pictures."

Now I was shocked and it took me a while to collect my thoughts.

" What sort of pictures?" I eventually asked.

" Me and Tom...doing things, he had one of those instant picture cameras, I was...I was...jeez I had him in my mouth, for God's sake Roo I was thirteen when he took them, I couldn't let my Dad see something like that."

I was lost for words, I was angry with her for doing things like that but I felt pity too because I knew she wouldn't have been willing, not at that age. I hated that bastard more than ever and vowed again that one day I would get even with him, not just for my sake but Alice's as well.

" You understand don't you?" Alice asked me

sadly, " Tom promised me the pictures if I would do this one thing for him. He said it was to prove that I loved him totally."

" Did you get the pictures?"

" Yes, all of them."

" Then why the fuck are you still with him?"

The question made perfect sense to me; Alice had no need to be with Tom any longer surely she could see that.

" Because I love him."

She gave me an answer that I was hoping not to hear. Love him? How could she? I felt the need to do something about it. Somehow I had to make her see sense, that it was pointless thinking she was in love with a bastard like Tom.

" How can you love him?" I asked, " He treats you so badly."

" He's dangerous, of course I know that," Alice replied, " but he fills me with so many different emotions, I don't think I could get that level of excitement anywhere else."

" But you've no experience of anyone else, you can't judge what real love is unless you've experienced other people."

" Why can't I? If I can get what I need from Tom, why would I need anyone else?"

I didn't know how to answer that and just blurted out,

" What about me?"

Alice stared and I turned my head away, speaking softly as I did so.

" You know how much I care about you."

Alice reached towards me with both hands and turned my head back until our eyes met.

" Oh Roo, I'm sorry, I need more than that and you deserve better than me. What do you think Tom would do to you if we got together? You know what he's capable of."

" I don't care, I want you."

I couldn't believe I had finally managed to say something I'd longed to say to Alice. I wanted to say more, I wanted to tell her I loved her. I wanted her to know everything I had ever felt about her, but I couldn't, I didn't have a chance to. Before I knew what she was doing I felt her mouth on mine. I was taken so completely by surprise I didn't know what to do, I didn't want to push her away so I didn't do anything. Alice pulled away and looked at me momentarily before lifting herself off the chair. She joined me on the floor reaching her arms around my shoulders and then giving me a little shove so that I fell backwards. In an instant she was lying on top of me and her mouth again locked onto mine. She flicked her tongue against my bottom lip and this time I responded. My lips parted, forced wider by her probing tongue. I'd never kissed anyone before and I was still unsure what to do. Alice withdrew her tongue from my mouth but kept her own lips open, I realised she wanted me to put my own tongue in, so I did. I felt completely useless; I hadn't got a clue what I was doing. I imagined myself as a naughty schoolboy poking my tongue out at a teacher. Alice pulled away so I guessed I was doing something wrong.

" Gently." she whispered, so I let her take control. Gradually I began to get the hang of it and soon I was giving back as good as I was getting. I was aware of the rest of my body becoming alive to what was happening and I felt embarrassed that Alice could probably feel the hardness of my groin pressing into her. She rolled off me and lay by my side, reaching out with her hand to touch the swelling in my jeans. I gasped out loud, everything was happening so fast. Alice flicked open the button of my trousers and swiftly pulled the zipper down. She slid her hand inside my pants and took hold of my penis. My body arched forwards at the sensation, it was such a shock, a million times better than my own hand. I felt I was going to ejaculate at once but then it was all over, Alice had let go. As I opened my eyes I could see her sitting up pulling her t-shirt over her head and revealing the bra that covered her breasts. I wanted to reach out and touch her but I was so terrified I just watched. Alice discarded her t-shirt and released the catch on her bra, I couldn't even begin to imagine the look on my face as her breasts tumbled into view but Alice just smiled at me and stood up. Her jeans and pants quickly followed and then she turned her attention to me. Kneeling down by my side Alice gripped the top of my jeans with both hands and pulled downwards, I raised my buttocks off the floor as she did so making her task that little bit easier. Alice had to move down between my feet to completely remove my trousers, letting out a murmour of satisfaction when my feet finally sprang free. On all fours, Alice slowly edged up my body, I could see her breasts hanging from her chest and I was so focused on them that I didn't realise she had removed my pants until she slowly dipped her head and kissed the tip of my penis. I was so shocked my whole body went rigid, my mind was racing, I couldn't understand or even believe we were in this situation, after all it was only a few minutes since she was telling me how much she loved Tom. I felt Alice take a couple of inches of me into her mouth and then pull away almost at once. For a split second I felt a little disappointed but it didn't last long as Alice moved to sit on my stomach. The flesh of her bottom felt cold against my skin and I was aware of my penis straining to reach her. Taking both my hands in hers, Alice drew them up and placed them on her breasts. I gave them a little squeeze, I didn't know what else I was meant to do. I wondered what Alice was thinking, even though I was convinced she thought I was completely useless, I hoped she wouldn't stop. I gave her breasts a firmer squeeze and sort of rubbed her nipples, hoping that what I was doing wasn't too ridiculous. Maybe it was because suddenly Alice climbed off me, removing my hands as she went, she slid over towards her jeans and for one horrible moment I thought that was it. One quick grope and goodbye. I wanted to scream 'don't go I can do better' but instead I just sat up and self-consciously covered my erection waiting for Alice to get dressed and disappear. I watched as she picked up her jeans and saw her hand reach into one of the pockets. When she took her hand out again I instantly recognised what it was she had been searching for.

" I thought you were going." I mumbled, as Alice moved back towards me ripping open the small foil package as she did so.

" And leave you like this?" she answered, taking hold of my penis and rolling the condom down its length, " what type of girl do you think I am?"
She laughed and I forced a smile as she pulled me

down on top of her, guiding me inside. It didn't last long but I don't think either of us expected it to. Selfishly I didn't care, this was my moment, this was my dream come true, I'd had sex with Alice.

CHAPTER NINE

We lay in each other's arms for ages afterwards. I didn't want to let go of her; I never wanted to let go...ever. For the rest of my life Alice would always be a part of me, she had taken my virginity. The horror of what had happened on my birthday, when I thought I had been screwing Alice, would forever play on my mind but I hadn't lost my innocence then, I had been raped so it didn't count. Alice had gone a long way to putting it right. I had understood her reasons for having to do what she did although there was no way that I could honestly say that I agreed with them. Now I realised that she must have been as tormented as much as I was afterwards and maybe her guilt had led her to do what we had just done. I wasn't complaining, quite the opposite in fact, I wanted to celebrate, shout it from the rooftops tell the whole world, but more than anything I wanted to do it again.

My returning hardness began to press at Alice's lower body and it was this that brought her back to reality. She had been lying quite content in my arms and now it seemed I had spoiled all that we had just shared. She pushed away from me and gave me such a look that I knew I had no chance of even kissing her again. I backed away from her and instinctively reached for her clothes offering them to her as a show of apology. We both quickly dressed not saying a word, neither of us quite knew what to say and before I knew it Alice was opening the front door. I desperately wanted to hold her in my arms and preach undying love for her.

" Alice." I started to say and she turned to look at me. Lifting her head upwards she kissed me lightly on the cheek whispering in my ear as she did so.

" I owed you that." was all she said and in an instant she was gone.

I called after her a few times but she never turned around. I rushed upstairs to look out of my bedroom window watching her for as long as possible before she vanished out of view, then I lay on my bed and buried my face in my pillow. I was a bit confused about Alice's reaction and her final words, maybe she had done it deliberately just to put her own guilt to rest or maybe I was being a little too cynical again, surely having sex with someone meant more to her than that. I made myself try to see things from her point of view but I couldn't. We had just had sex, it was the ultimate act between two people and she had just run away. I was convinced that the whole morning had been pointless, nothing had changed. I still needed to talk to Alice, even more than ever but I knew she wouldn't be calling round again. It was time for me to venture outside.

CHAPTER TEN

It was yet another night on which I didn't get much sleep and I was extremely tired the next day. My head had been spinning more than ever. All the time I was awake I was thinking of Alice and all the time I was asleep I was dreaming of her. I was determined that this was the day that I would start to put my life back together and that would mean meeting up with Tom and the rest. I had to, it was probably the only way I would see Alice again.

It was mid morning before I ventured downstairs, Dad had long gone to work and Mum was busy with her chores. I asked her if she needed anything from the shops, I saw it as an excuse for me to take my first steps outside. Mum looked surprised at my suggestion and tried to decline my offer of help but I was insistent and she finally agreed that I could go for her. She told me what she wanted and thrust some money into my hands. There was no going back for me now. I put on my shoes and coat and headed out of the door.

My heart was beating in anticipation as I made my way down the road towards the local shops.

PUTTING IT RIGHT

Everything about the estate was as I remembered it, not that I had expected it to change. There weren't many people around but even so I felt they were all looking at me. I felt a stranger in my own town. I imagined everybody peering out from behind their curtains, each and every one of them knowing what had happened to me. I was sure there were rumours and counter rumours flying around because I hadn't been seen for so long but I consoled myself with the fact that no one could possibly know the truth. Occasionally I bumped into someone I knew, mainly friends of my parents, and I exchanged small talk with them. The more I actually spoke to people the more confident I became, perhaps no one was really that bothered that I hadn't been seen.

I felt a sense of relief when I arrived at the small shopping precinct and I couldn't see anyone that I used to hang around with. I glanced at my watch and noted that it was lunchtime and that meant the fish and chip shop would soon be attracting one or two of them as it dealt with the lunchtime trade. I hurried around the few shops collecting the items that Mum wanted before pausing in the square of the precinct. I felt hungry and checked the change from the money that my mother had given me. Good, there was just enough left for a small bag of chips.

I went inside the takeaway, turning my nose up at the stench of fish, and gave my order. At least the chips were fresh at this time of day and not like early evening when the first load were re-cooked from lunchtime. I watched as one of the three assistants added salt and vinegar to my food before I took it outside to eat. I settled onto one of the benches in the square, putting my shopping bags on the ground between my feet, before tucking into my lunchtime snack.

It wasn't long before I noticed Tom and Alice coming into view. I wasn't sure if Alice was bunking off school or just meeting Tom for lunch. It didn't matter either way because the surge of jealousy I felt seeing the two of them together took away any reason I was pondering for her being there. I had to remain as composed as I possibly could but the fear of the impending situation made me choke on the mouthful of chips I was trying to swallow. Until that moment I don't think Tom had noticed me but my involuntary act had managed to draw his attention to me. My coughing subsided and as I looked up I could see him making his way towards me, laughing. Alice was tugging at his jacket sleeve attempting to stop him but Tom wasn't going to miss such an opportunity. Strangely, because of Alice's reaction, I was ready for him and with a show of nonchalance I popped another chip into my mouth just as Tom reached me.

" Leave it Tom."

I could barely hear Alice's words I was concentrating on Tom so hard. He reached into my paper grabbed a handful of chips and lowered his head until his face was an inch from mine. He spat out a single word.

" Queer."

I was expecting a lot more but it was just one word and then he stood up with a sense of triumph before screwing up the handful of chips and throwing them into my face. I longed to stand up for myself and say something back, even more so after what had happened between me and Alice, but I couldn't risk putting Alice in a position she couldn't deal with. I didn't know how Tom would react to either of us and I thought it more likely that he would seek revenge on Alice more than me. I knew I wouldn't be able to live with myself if anything happened to her because of something I had said.

Alice managed to push Tom away from me and towards the takeaway and once she had got him inside came back to see me.

" I'm sorry," she said as I was disposing my unfinished chips in the dustbin next to the bench. I don't know what came over me but without thinking I went to give Alice a kiss on the lips. She backed off in horror.

" No... not here!" she said quickly, her voice agitated as she looked back towards the chip shop. I instantly realised what I had almost done.

" Sorry, but I've got to see you." I said apologetically.

" Me too," Alice agreed and before I had time to react continued, " tonight...seven o'clock...school sports hut..."

She hurried off back to Tom leaving me open mouthed in complete astonishment. I had expected her to tell me to leave her alone not arrange to meet me. I had to be there, I hadn't been given a chance to say yes or no. I picked up my bags of shopping and rushed out of the precinct not daring to look in the direction of Alice and Tom as I passed the shop window. I was out of breath when I reached the front gate of my house and momentarily paused to regain a bit of self-control. When my breathing had steadied I made my way indoors giving my mother a huge grin as I handed over the shopping. I was proud of myself for finally making the first step on the journey back to a life of normality.

CHAPTER ELEVEN

I didn't know what I expected that night from Alice but I was going to make sure that I looked my best. Remembering what she had said to me earlier made me think that our tryst was going to have a positive outcome but I couldn't be totally sure so I decided that looking good could only help the situation. I told Mum that I was going out that evening and that led to a pretty in depth question and answer session although it was more questions than answers as I couldn't tell her the whole truth. In fact I didn't really tell her anything that she believed, it was just that I had to go out sometime and that night was as good a time as any. I would have loved to tell her that I was meeting Alice and that she was now my girlfriend but that was still just my dream. I knew that Mum and Dad found Alice a bit 'tarty and cheap' but they didn't know her like I did. I smiled inwardly as I imagined them walking in on me and Alice yesterday morning, that certainly wouldn't have changed their opinion of her but that was their problem, I was crazy about her.

Meeting Alice at seven didn't give me a lot of time

to get ready. I decided to leave around six because I wanted to get there before her, it wasn't as though I didn't trust her, I knew that she wouldn't ever set me up again, I just wanted a big enough time lapse so that if anyone saw me they wouldn't realise that I was meeting up with Alice.

I had an early tea at around four thirty and when I had finished I headed off to the bathroom. Over the past few weeks I had begun to develop a phobia about the bathroom and having a bath. I knew it was a little bit silly but it was the one place in my house that brought back the painful memory of the events of my birthday to the forefront of my mind. Things were different this time; I had a positive reason for getting clean. Even when I was lying back soaking amongst the bubbles not once did I think about trying to scrape away the dirt of that night. I even burst into song, some over-romantic slushy pop record that was high in the music chart. I lay there until the water cooled then climbed out. I wrapped the towel around my body and went over to the mirror that was hanging above the sink. I wiped away the condensation and looked at my reflection. I contemplated having a shave but after looking at myself soon realised that there wasn't anything there that warranted the possible mutilation of my face for. I chuckled at the thought of going out with countless bits of cotton wool stuck to my chin, that would create a lasting impression on Alice. I reached into the bathroom cabinet and pulled out a bottle of Dad's aftershave lotion. At least that would create an illusion of having shaved I thought. I also thought that maybe I was trying too hard, but I splashed some on anyway.

I made my way down the landing and into my bedroom where I hastily dried myself before opening the wardrobe door and selecting what I was going to wear. My best shirt and a decent pair of trousers, I wasn't fashionable by any stretch of the imagination and I didn't have the popular shirts and trousers that were currently in favour. It wasn't that I didn't want to be trendy, it was just that my parents couldn't afford such luxuries. I never complained because to me it wasn't that important.

As I got dressed it dawned on me that it didn't even matter what I was wearing because it would all be hidden underneath my duffle coat and that meant that Alice wouldn't see the effort I had gone to. I could always use a little more aftershave.

I glanced at my watch, I had ten minutes before I had to leave, I wandered over to the window and looked out. It was getting quite dark which to me was good as it meant I was less likely to be noticed. It was going to be cold waiting for Alice to turn up so I considered putting a t-shirt on underneath my shirt but when I pulled open my draw I saw instead a jumper that my nan had knitted for me just before she passed away. I had never worn it before and didn't particularly like it but I put it on anyway. It was time to go, I felt a little apprehensive but it wasn't a time for getting cold feet. It was Alice's idea to meet and I wasn't going to let her down.

I made my way downstairs, grabbing my coat from the rack just inside the door. Shouting goodbye I shut the door firmly behind me. I didn't hear any response from Mum or Dad nor did I want to. They would only have made a fuss and that was something I could do without. It would take me about fifteen minutes to reach my destination and then another forty minutes or so for Alice to arrive. I began to feel a bit stupid for going so early but there was no turning back. I walked briskly to keep out the night's chilly air and arrived at the school in good time. The caretaker had padlocked the gate so I climbed over. The caretaker's house was in the opposite direction to where I was going. I doubted that he would be wandering around the grounds and anyway there was never any trouble around the school at nighttime. Even Tom and his mates never bothered to come down as it was too far from their usual haunts.

I made my way through the numerous outside classrooms and on towards the rear of the main school building where the sports fields were. At the far end of the field was the sports hut where I was to meet Alice. I was grateful that there hadn't been any rain over the past few days as that meant the field wouldn't be its usual sodden mess. I didn't like sports much, mainly because it was used as an excuse by my fellow pupils to get me as filthy as possible. Rugby was the worst and I always seemed to be at the bottom of a ruck even when the ball had long gone. I shuddered at the thought that I would be going back to school soon and that it was still part of the rugby season. I hoped I could get permission to be excused from P.E. for the remainder of my time at school but I didn't think it likely and it would probably add to my chances of physical and verbal abuse. I decided I would just get on with the last few months of school as best I could.

I reached the sports hut and sat down on one of the wooden benches that were positioned on either side of the doors. I was sweating a little from my walk but resisted the urge to remove my coat. I looked back across the field towards the school and waited for Alice to arrive. There was no other way to get to where I was sat so if anyone else turned up I would see them first.

I was worrying needlessly because at five to seven Alice duly appeared, alone.

It took barely thirty seconds for her to walk across the playing field to join me at the hut. She greeted me amiably as she got close and bent down and kissed me lightly on the cheek when she reached me. She sat down next to me pushing herself up really close and rested her hand on my thigh. I wasn't quite sure if she was getting close because she was cold or because she was genuinely pleased to be in my company. I decided it was a bit of both because it suited me to think like that and I wasn't going to complain because it meant her body was touching mine. We sat quietly for a while, both of us not knowing what to say, a sort of awkward silence until for me it turned into one of those moments when you wish you hadn't opened your mouth.

" You not seeing Tom tonight?"

I heard the words coming out of my mouth but I couldn't do anything to stop them. I quickly glanced at Alice and saw the look of disappointment etched on her face.

" I'm sorry," I stammered placing my hand on top of hers. She didn't move it and inwardly I gave myself a huge sigh of relief, " what I mean is," I continued, " I hope you don't have to go too soon."

Alice shifted her position on the bench so that she was facing me and we looked into each other's eyes. Even though I was alone with her I couldn't help wishing that somehow I was able to whisk her off to a faraway place where no one knew us.

" I didn't sleep last night," Alice broke her silence, her voice was soft but assured, " all I could do was think of you, about what happened."

" Me too." was all I managed in reply. I thought for one moment that she was going to tell me that it was all a mistake, that that was it, a one off, something never to be repeated, but she didn't.

" I want to carry on seeing you."

They were words I had been longing to hear but I was still so completely taken aback I wanted to run away. As ever I had absolutely no confidence in myself and my ability to deal with girls I liked or in particular, Alice. It wasn't as though I couldn't talk to them, I could, but only as if they were friends. I had this enviable talent to make the opposite sex laugh but once feelings progressed beyond friendship I became completely flustered and started talking gibberish. It was as though I didn't want to say anything foolish yet it was by being foolish that I had made them laugh. I didn't understand myself sometimes so how could I imagine that they would.

This was turning into a really intimidating experience for me. Here I was on the brink of a relationship with someone I was totally in love with and I couldn't find a single word to say. I imagined that Alice would be having second thoughts about wanting to carry on seeing the imbecile in front of her. Inside my head I was desperately trying to put together a rational statement that would not only make sense to Alice but to me as well. But instead of saying anything that Alice would probably want to hear, I managed to put my foot in it again.

" What are we going to tell Tom?" I asked.

I knew straight away it was the wrong question, the look of exasperation on Alice's face told me that. Too late I realised that this moment was about Alice and me and had nothing to do with Tom. Still, it was a question that had to be answered sometime and now that I had asked it I expected an honest reply.

" For God's sake Roo," Alice began, " I've just said I wanted to carry on seeing you. Just kiss me."

" But..." I started to say, I couldn't finish as Alice thrust her face onto mine and our lips locked.

I tried to pull away but Alice was having none of it and putting her hands behind my head held me so that I couldn't move. I had no choice but to give in to her soft moist mouth. Alice was being really forceful and I supposed that she was trying to give the impression of how much she really wanted me. We kissed and tasted each other for ages, barely drawing breath and I was pleased how much I had improved since my first fumbled attempts of the previous morning. Eventually our lips parted and we cuddled up together.

" I'm not going to stop seeing Tom," Alice finally said, " I've told you how much he means to me and he's the man I'm going to marry, but at this moment in time I want to see you as well."

She looked at me with a saddened expression and I don't know how she expected me to answer. I felt hurt but I was already resigned to the fact that Tom wasn't going to be dumped in favour of me. I had to make a decision and it seemed I had to make it quickly. I didn't want to lose Alice, I had only just got her into my life, but could I share her with someone I detested so much. I had no choice, I had to say yes.

CHAPTER TWELVE

The next six months were the best of my relatively short life. Alice and I had so much fun. The secrecy of our relationship made it all the more exciting, dangerous even. I suffered more than usual for the first few weeks at the hands of Tom and his friends but knowing that I was seeing Alice behind his back gave me a smug sense of satisfaction and I was able to deal with the verbal abuse with disdain. I knew I could never tell him what I was doing as Alice had begged me not to and I would never have done anything to hurt her. I wasn't Tom, he still treated her like dirt on many occasions but even those times, from a selfish point of view, were good because it seemed to push Alice and I closer together.

I duly went back to school after Christmas and did the best I could. I was fortunate to be able to leave at Easter provided I had a job to go to and much to my parents dismay I managed to fill a vacancy at the local fish and chip shop. It wasn't anything like the trade my parents had hoped for but for me it was a means to an end because it meant that I could see Alice virtually every day. Whether it was because I was seeing her or the passage of time, I had managed to become fully in control of my life.

My parents were delighted by my transformation and were hopeful that my new found confidence might even lead to me getting what they called a proper job. How disappointed they would have been if they knew that my happiness was all due to Alice.

I worked six days a week from Monday til Saturday, altering my shifts between lunchtimes and evenings. Lunchtimes were the best for seeing Alice because Tom wasn't always with her. We would chat for ages about anything and everything and arrange times when we could meet alone. If I knew Mum was going out I would arrange my shift to work late so that Alice and I could spend the morning in bed. I loved making love with Alice and she taught me so much. From the fumbling and embarrassment that I felt when we had so unexpectedly first had sex, I had become more and more self assured in what I was doing, although in the back of my mind, because Alice had been doing it since she was thirteen, I didn't think I could teach her anything. It bothered me greatly that Alice had learnt what she was now teaching me from Tom and sometimes when I saw them together it was hard to control my jealousy. If I was at work and saw them coming I would disappear out the back of the shop for a coffee break, hanging around long enough for them to get their food and leave.

I was no longer intimidated by Tom or any of the others and over the months their victimisation of me began to dwindle. The insults over my sexual orientation continued though and what I would have given to be able to put them in their place with stories of Alice and me. But I didn't or rather couldn't so I just took their insults on board as best I could. It took a while but eventually they all began to realise that I wasn't going to let it bother me and slowly but surely I was virtually accepted into their group. I was always going to be the fall guy but I'd been the one they had picked on for as long as I could remember.

The summer came and we all spent a lot of time together just loafing around. My blossoming confidence had renewed my sense of humour and I was beginning to make a few of Tom's friends laugh with my one-liners. I was never going to be close friends with any of them after what they had done but I thought if I could get them to laugh with me then my life would be almost perfect. Tom would never laugh though, he'd look at me through cold eyes because I was taking the attention away from him, but I didn't honestly care, I despised him as much as ever.

Alice's sixteenth birthday was in August and even though our relationship was special what she did that day filled me with tremendous pride. It may not have seemed much to many people but to me it was a million times better than when we'd first had sex.

I had wanted that day to be memorable for her and with some money I had put by from my wages I had bought her a necklace. I had arranged to meet her early in the morning so that I could give her my present and depending on her reaction to it was going to ask her to finally end it with Tom. I had already made sure that Mum would be out that day and Alice arrived at my house at nine thirty. She seemed so pleased to see me when she burst through the door that I was slightly put off my stride. I handed over my gift to her, wishing her a happy birthday and she excitedly tore off the wrapping paper before opening the box. I was thrilled at how impressed she was with it and offered to fasten it around her neck.

" Thanks," she enthused, " and then I've got a gift for you."

" Don't be silly," I laughed, " it's your birthday, why would you be giving me anything?"

Alice laughed out really loud at my choice of words and then clasped my hands in hers looking at me seriously before saying,

" I've reached the age of consent and I want you to be the first."

I was astounded and stood there open mouthed for ages before what she had said hit me, and then I broke into what was probably the biggest smile I had ever given in my life. It didn't matter any more what had happened to us or between us in the past, this was going to be the defining moment of our relationship.

Alice looked at the huge grin on my face and smiling back at me briefly, raced upstairs with me following closely behind. I don't think we had ever laughed so much as we ripped the clothes from our bodies and had the most frantic sex we had ever had. It was fantastic, it couldn't get any better, we were made for each other.

" Leave Tom." I said afterwards as we lay under the sheets teasing each other's body with gentle caresses.

" Please don't ask me Roo, not now, let's not spoil this."

I for once understood what she meant, why bring the image of Tom into such a tender intimate moment.

CHAPTER THIRTEEN

Tom took Alice out that night; I saw them from the takeaway window. Alice sneaked a glimpse over to where I stood watching, she looked so beautiful. One day soon I hoped it would be me stood there with her and that Tom would be a distant memory. Despite the fact that we hadn't even discussed her leaving Tom I was secretly hoping that she could do it soon maybe even that night. I was convinced that she was going to do it and it made the fact that she was holding his hand just a little bit more bearable. I wished I didn't have to witness their shows of affection but was resigned to the knowledge that I couldn't do anything about it.

I saw the bus that was to take them further into town pull up at the stop. Not wanting to see them depart I turned back towards the shop counter. We hadn't been busy with customers so far and I was hoping that trade would pick up so I could take my mind off Alice being with Tom.

I muddled through the rest of my shift, as it turned out it was hardly worth staying open for the amount of trade we had and I was constantly clock watching. Part of me wanted Alice and Tom to stop for something to eat on the way home but when the time came to shut up shop they hadn't appeared.

At about eleven thirty, after cleaning up, it was time for me to make the walk home. I was last to leave because it was my turn to lock up. The other staff had said their goodbyes about thirty minutes earlier. I closed the door behind me as I left and locked it, popping the key into my trouser pocket. Turning away from the shop I strolled across the square. Despite the time of night it was still quite warm and I was glad because I only had on a thin cotton shirt. I turned left and walked up the slight hill towards the George, crossing the road as I went. I couldn't hear anybody in the vicinity of the pub which was just as well because I didn't want any trouble, all I wanted to do was get home and go to bed. I stank of the smells of frying but a bath would have to wait until the morning, it wouldn't be fair to disturb my parents at such a late hour.

I quickened my stride as I headed up the hill making my way towards the playground. It wouldn't take too long to reach the end of the main road and then turn right towards the estate on which I lived.

" Roo."

I heard the voice call out as I passed the

playground entrance. I thought it was coming from behind me and I turned back to have a look. There was no one there. Slightly puzzled I looked ahead of myself again but could still see no one.

" Roo."

The voice called again and was a little louder this time. I realised that it was coming from inside the playground. As I looked, a figure appeared from behind the hedge beside the entrance gate. I didn't recognise her at first because she stayed in the shadows but the harder I stared into the darkness I soon realised it was Alice.

" Hi, what are you doing here?" I said smiling broadly, believing that she had purposely been waiting to be with me.

" Come here." Alice spoke quietly and it sounded like she was crying. I immediately pushed open the iron gate and went over to her. She moved back behind the hedge turning her face away from me.

" What's wrong?" I asked anxiously and reached out to turn her back around to face me.

" Oh shit!" I was shocked by what I saw; Alice's face was a mess. It was covered in scratches and showing signs of severe bruising.

" How the hell did that happen?" I exclaimed, my immediate thoughts were that Tom had done it in a fit of rage after Alice had told him about us.

I began to get angry.

" I'm going to fucking kill him," I shouted, " the bastard, how dare he do this to you."

I'd known that Tom had hit Alice before because she had told me but it was always on parts of the body that couldn't be seen. This time he had gone too far.

" Do you know where he is?" I snapped at Alice who by now was crying her eyes out. The look on her face changed my mood at once; I was reacting in the wrong manner. I was being like Tom, aggressive, when I should have been comforting her. I pulled her towards me wrapping both my arms around her body, squeezing her tightly. I hadn't given her a chance to explain. I was jumping to conclusions just assuming that it was Tom who had hurt her. It couldn't have been anyone else though could it? Maybe someone had attacked her while she was waiting for me. The playground was opposite the pub, what if someone had been watching her waiting. I had to calm myself down and wait until Alice was ready to talk. By the state of her, whatever had happened must have been terrifying for her. I remembered my own experience of almost twelve months ago when I had no one to help me through it. I couldn't afford to make things worse by seeking out Tom for any sort of retribution, I had to put Alice's feelings first.

We held each other tight until her crying had given away to gentle sobs. I had comforted her as best I could, telling her that everything would be alright, that I would always be there for her. I couldn't be sure that she was listening to a single word I was saying but by the way she was clinging on to me I knew she was glad to have me there.

It took the best part of an hour for Alice to relax sufficiently enough for us to be able to move to one of the playground benches. We had stood in the same spot the whole time and as my feet were getting quite numb I presumed that Alice's were too. I tried to release my grip on her but she was having none of it so we had to move awkwardly across the grass to where the bench was before we could sit down.

" What happened Alice?" I asked again, kissing her gently on the forehead as I waited for her to reply.

" It was my fault."

I couldn't believe Alice's answer, how could she even think about blaming herself. I felt the anger welling up inside me again but I restrained myself from saying anything as she continued.

" We'd been to a couple of pubs in town and we both had lots to drink. Tom was being so nice to me," her words were interrupted as she started to cry again. As much as I wanted to hear what he had done I told her to stop but she wouldn't. " He was being so nice, like never before, I kept thinking of you and my head was spinning so much I couldn't cope."

She paused for a moment, pulling away from me and held her head in her hands.

" I'd had one drink too many," the tone of her voice was more assertive like she was becoming angry. I hoped she wasn't still blaming herself and that her anger would be directed at Tom. " I didn't feel well, I needed to get outside for some fresh air to clear my head, I needed space. Tom followed me outside because he thought I was going to be sick. I told him to leave me alone and he took it the wrong way. He got upset and called me selfish."

" So why didn't you just come home?"

" I wanted to, I asked him to bring me back but he said he was staying for another pint."

" You could have left him couldn't you?"

" I wish I had, but I followed him back inside the pub and yelled at him that it was all over unless he took me home."

" You could have phoned me at work, you know the number, I would have come for you."

" He would have loved that, anyway he knew I was serious and came with me trying as hard as he could to make up. We got off the bus and ended up here. He wanted sex but I said no, I...I should have said yes, then he wouldn't have forced me, he went crazy he said I should never turn him down. I tried to fight him off but he kept hitting me until I could fight no more. When he had finished he just ran off and left me."

" Jesus Alice, I'm so sorry." I didn't know what else to say. I had disliked Tom for a long time but now it was pure hatred. Everything he had ever done to me had become irrelevant, he could not be allowed to get away with what he had done to Alice. He hadn't paid for the rape of me but he sure as hell was going to pay for raping Alice.

" You mustn't tell anyone about this," Alice spoke through gritted teeth, " it was all my fault."

" No way, it's got to be sorted, he raped you Alice." I was determined that she would see that I was right.

" No!" Alice was adamant, " it's done with, I don't want people knowing, I'll talk to him."

" You can't even think about seeing him again." I voiced my opinion strongly to Alice but she remained resolute and no amount of persuasion could get her to change her mind. I had to accept that it was her decision to make and had nothing to do with me.

I looked at my watch and saw that it was fast

approaching one o'clock in the morning. My parents wouldn't have been worried at my being out so late because I'd often been later home from work than I'd planned. I wasn't sure about Alice's Mum and Dad though but I guessed she'd been out later quite often.

" You can stay at my house tonight if you don't want to go home." I said without thinking.

" What about your parents, won't they mind?" Alice asked.

" They won't need to know, you can stay with me for as long as you like. You need to stay somewhere until your face has healed if you don't want anybody to see and start asking questions."

Alice was very unsure about my suggestion but eventually I managed to convince her that it was the perfect solution and she finally agreed to come with me. She told me that she had stayed at Tom's for weeks at a time before and she felt that she could use it as an excuse for not going home. I was due some holiday from work and decided to use the days off staying at home making sure Alice wasn't discovered. It wouldn't be an easy thing to achieve especially as Mum didn't go out too often but Alice needed to be protected and it also meant that Tom wouldn't have any idea where she was. I could see that this incident would give me the chance to spend time with Alice and hopefully persuade her to get rid of Tom for good.

As we left the playground we nervously looked both ways out of the gate. I was equally concerned about the whereabouts of Tom but surmised that if he was about he would have caused no end of problems had he seen me with Alice. It didn't take long to reach my house and Alice promised to be as quiet as possible so that if anyone stirred they wouldn't realise that there were two of us. We sneaked upstairs to my bedroom and I pushed a couple of boxes up against the door to stop anyone coming in without me knowing. We then stripped off our clothes in the darkness and climbed under the sheets on my bed. Alice snuggled up close and it was wonderful to feel her skin against mine. She fell asleep almost at once but I lay awake most of the night, listening just in case.

CHAPTER FOURTEEN

Mum was up and out early in the morning and I took advantage of her absence to change the layout of my bedroom, moving the furniture around to create a space in which Alice could disappear if necessary. While I was busy upstairs Alice made a phone-call to her parents to tell them of her plans to stay with Tom. Even though she was lying she knew they wouldn't try and get in touch with her through Tom, he wasn't good enough for their daughter and though they couldn't stop her from seeing him at his house, he was never allowed to set foot in theirs. Alice didn't have to be back at school for another three weeks so it didn't matter what day she returned home.

When she had finished with the phone I called work and arranged time off, they weren't best pleased with me but I told them it was a family crisis and something I couldn't get out of so they reluctantly agreed to let me have as much time as I needed.

I managed to put Alice's dirty clothes through the washing machine and in the meantime she wore some of mine. We went through the kitchen cupboards together to make a stockpile of rations to last for however long Alice was to stay upstairs. Afterwards I ran her a bath and sat with her as she washed her troubles away.

She didn't look too bad when she had finished but I still reckoned that the bruising would probably take about ten days to fade. Alice didn't think she could stay that long but I reminded her that she didn't have much choice. I promised I would make everything as normal for her as I possibly could. I knew her emotions were going to be all over the place but at least I had the opportunity to be there for her.

We settled into what was going to be Alice's home just before Mum came back, the washing machine had just finished its spin cycle and I quickly bundled the damp clothes into my arms and rushed upstairs before Mum came through the door. I turned my radio on to drown out any noise that we might make and left Alice alone for a few minutes. We had already devised a code for me to be singing loudly when I came upstairs so that she needn't panic every time she heard a noise. Most of the time I would be with her anyway.

I greeted Mum in the kitchen saying that I had a few days off work and asked her what was for tea as I was really hungry and could she cook a little extra.

" You're probably missing all the chips you eat at work," she laughed.

It wasn't going to be easy smuggling hot food upstairs but I had to try. I needed some excuses at mealtimes to be able to wander into the kitchen so that neither Mum nor Dad could see what I was up to. I couldn't do it every day otherwise they might get suspicious and the consequences of that would almost certainly lead them to Alice. I decided I would wash and dry the dishes every night to give me another opportunity to put together a meal for my hidden guest.

I left Mum to the prospect of cooking and returned to Alice, stupidly I forgot I was meant to sing and when I entered the room Alice was nowhere to be seen. I said sorry to her for my mistake but pointed out that the hideaway had worked well. It didn't seem to placate her and it was then that I noticed she was shaking. I realised just how vulnerable she was and felt really guilty, it was going to be a tough few days.

Alice coped well for the remainder of the day and I'd managed to get some food for her on the pretext that I was going to the toilet. It wasn't a huge amount but understandably she didn't feel much like eating. There was however the ration box under my bed which contained crisps, biscuits and fruit, so if she got her appetite back later then there was plenty to tuck into.

I said goodnight to my parents quite early and wandered upstairs singing as loudly as I could. I pushed open the door just wide enough for me to get through and glanced behind me to check that no one was following. Alice had hid behind the door when I went in, just in case, she said.

I closed the door, blocking it again with the boxes and turned the radio on. Alice had curled up on the bed so I sat on the floor beside her and ran my fingers across her shoulders and through her hair. She looked at me forlornly for a while, like a little lost child, but then gave me a smile. I smiled back.

" I love you so much Alice." I said.

" I know." she replied and closed her eyes.

The next few days were pretty much the same except that we talked a lot more. I began to feel that we were becoming firm friends as well as lovers and that nothing would ever split us up. Until the fifth night that Alice had stayed with me we had only cuddled up to each other in bed but that night Alice said that she felt like making love. Her bruised body was recovering rapidly and she wasn't in as much pain as on previous days. She had always been the one who sorted out our contraception but because of the way she had arrived at my house, didn't have any with her. I was far too shy to be able to buy any myself so it was lucky for me that one day I'd come across some while I was snooping around in my parents bedroom. I was only fourteen at the time and was a little curious so I pinched two or three to experiment with. They must have noticed that some were missing and that it was me who had taken them but they never said anything about it. I masturbated into one of them and it had felt so horrible that I hid the others away; I didn't dare put them back.

I searched them out from their hiding place and got into bed with Alice, she was already naked and it wasn't long before I was too. It was a strange experience holding our breath hardly daring to move in case we were overheard but we managed it and it was a great relief for both of us.

It wasn't going to be easy from now on to control myself; I only had one condom left and no chance of going out to get some more. I toyed with the idea of raiding Dad's draw but even though I'd done it before it just didn't seem right. In a month I would be seventeen and it was about time I started taking more responsibility for the way I lived my life. I wasn't a boy any more.

It was on the ninth day that Alice left, she had been getting more and more restless over the previous twenty-four hours. I knew she was missing her parents and although it was a wrench for me to see her go it also meant I was able to get outside again. I needed to get back to work because I didn't want to lose my job so I was pleased that Alice's injuries had healed sufficiently for her to be able to go home without anyone any the wiser to what had happened and where she had really been. It would always remain our secret. It didn't bother me what Tom thought or what he had been up to whilst we'd been hidden away, Alice and I both knew he wouldn't have searched her out at her house because of the friction between him and Alice's parents. There weren't many adults on our estate who actually liked him or his family a great deal so I doubted he had any idea that Alice hadn't been staying at her own home.

She left mid-morning and we said a tearful goodbye to each other. Under the circumstances of being trapped in one room we had had a pretty good time. I felt closer to her than I had ever done. Soon Tom would be nothing but a distant memory as Alice would have no choice but to end their relationship. If she had any sense she would tell the police what had happened and maybe then my Dad's prophesy would come true and Tom would end up inside.

Either way it meant at long last Alice and I could be a proper couple and get on with spending the rest of our lives together.

CHAPTER FIFTEEN

I didn't see much of Alice alone over the next two weeks. I had returned to work and she had gone back to school. She said she was determined to work a lot harder during her final year and maybe get a qualification or two. I knew she had the ability but wasn't so sure about her willpower especially if Tom got his claws into her again.

I knew she was still seeing him because I had seen them together a few times albeit from a distance as they had stopped coming into the shop when I was working. I found it hard to understand how she could return to his arms after what he had done to her, she hadn't even mentioned his name all the time she had stayed with me and I had thought that was because she had etched him from her memory. I found myself getting a little upset about the situation and on days when I didn't even see a glimpse of her I tortured myself as to what she was getting up to. What made things even harder was the fact that it was fast approaching my birthday bringing back all the dreadful memories of the previous year. I really needed Alice with me, helping me through it but it was difficult to talk to someone you didn't see. I was sure she wasn't avoiding me on purpose but that's what it felt like.

The week before my birthday I didn't see her at all and I began sinking into despair. I was becoming short tempered with those around me and it was beginning to affect my work, once resulting in my being rude to customers just because I was having a bad day mentally. I was starting to think I would never see her again when finally the day before my birthday she came into the shop. I was delighted to see her but she didn't seem as pleased to see me. Somehow she just wasn't the Alice I knew, something was troubling her.

" I need to talk to you," she said as I asked her what was wrong.

We agreed to meet the following day before my shift at work started and for me it couldn't come quickly enough. There was so much I needed to ask her about. We'd had such a good time when she stayed with me that I couldn't understand her current coldness. It wasn't as though I'd done anything wrong.

I was on edge the next morning but managed not to let it show to Mum and Dad as they presented me with the gifts they had bought. Despite the money shortage they had really gone out of their way to make it a special day for me. I felt bad about having to go out early after their kindness but meeting Alice was so important. I'd agreed to meet her at the end of my road and walk her to school. She was already waiting when I strolled up but as I went to give her a kiss on the cheek she pulled away. This wasn't a good sign and I immediately expected the worst but what she said took me completely by surprise.

" I'm pregnant."

I was stunned, my first reaction was that it was mine but I couldn't think how, we had always used protection. It must have been that old one of Dad's that we used.

" It's Tom's." Alice continued, turning back to look at me because I had stopped walking.

" But... how?" I didn't know if I was disappointed, I really didn't know what I felt because I hadn't anticipated hearing what Alice was telling me. She started giving me all the details, including stuff I didn't want to hear. Ever since the first time with Tom when she was thirteen they hadn't used condoms because he didn't like them. To me that showed just how much he was using her, what would he have done if she had fallen pregnant at that age, forced her into an abortion? I was getting angry inside and I felt nauseous. What was Alice doing to me, didn't she realise what day it was, didn't she realise how fucked up I was and that something like this would only make it worse. I ran off up the road only stopping to lean over a garden wall to throw up, I was crying, I didn't think life was worth living any more. I couldn't bear not to be with Alice.

She caught up with me and put her arm around my shoulder.

" I'm sorry Roo, but you had to know. It's why I haven't been around much lately. I had to get my head straight, I didn't know what to say to you. I was falling in love with you, I really was."

Alice was tearful as well; I wanted to give her a hug but couldn't bring myself to do it.

" How long?" I had to ask the question, maybe she had made a mistake and the baby was mine after all.

" Almost three months."

" So you knew all the time you stayed with me?" I said indignantly.

" No! I found out after I left," she sounded exasperated, " you don't think I could lie to you?"

" You've lied to me before." I knew that would annoy her and I didn't really mean to say it.

" That wasn't my fault, you know that," she snapped back before adding, " oh Roo, I'm sorry, I've just remembered what day it is."

But it was already too late for me, I had to get

away, I had to be on my own. There were questions I had to ask myself before I could speak to Alice again so I left her standing there. I could hear her calling after me but I chose to ignore her and carried on walking.

We only met up once after that, about five or six days later. It was a highly charged emotional few hours. We ended up making love and it was on Alice's insistence that I didn't wear a condom. We both knew it would be for the last time and Alice wanted us to do it 'properly' as she put it. It should have been the perfect moment but it didn't feel right to me, I felt I was just going through the motions and couldn't relax enough to enjoy it. I was having sex with the only girl I would ever truly love and she was carrying someone else's child. We parted amicably enough but inside I was completely torn apart. I had lost Alice forever and I was heading for a breakdown and even though I knew it, I couldn't do anything to stop it.

I began to drink heavily, hanging around the George nearly every day. I lost my job because I couldn't be bothered to go to work. I spent all my unemployment benefit on alcohol. Everything was everybody else's fault but mine and I got into many fights including one with Tom. I hated that bastard more than ever and I had to be dragged off him before I went too far. I was still protective of my relationship with Alice and as much as I wanted him to know I kept my mouth shut.

Alice tried her best to remain friends and I did speak to her but she had broken my heart and the pain was so great that it wasn't possible to talk to her the way I used to, the way I wanted to.

Christmas came and went and I was in a complete mess, much worse than I had ever been during the weeks immediately after the day I'd been raped. My parents by this time were totally distraught by what was going on. Everything they tried to do to help was rejected out of hand. They knew it was something to do with Alice and they knew she was pregnant, I had enough comments from them about being lucky not to have ended up with someone like her.

" What do you know," I shouted at them, " you haven't got a fucking clue."

I had taken things a bit too far with them and they wanted me out of their home. I knew I couldn't sink any lower and I thought about ending it all. Sitting alone in my room crying my eyes out clutching a bottle of pills all I could do was think of Alice. She was due to give birth any day and I think the thought of that was what stopped me from swallowing the tablets. Maybe just maybe there was a glimmer of hope that the baby was mine. I knew I had to see it just to make sure. It was the only way I could come to terms with my life and even think about moving on. I vowed to make my peace with everyone, everyone except Tom.

CHAPTER SIXTEEN

I was in the George when Tom came in to announce loudly the news of the birth of his son. He spotted me almost immediately and couldn't resist the opportunity to try and provoke me.

" Reynolds," he shouted so that the whole pub went quiet and all the regulars could hear everything he was saying, " I've done something you will never do...I've become a father."
He laughed believing he was being so amusing but I didn't react. I turned away from him and carried on drinking. Even though I was only seventeen I had no problems being served alcohol, I drank enough for the landlord to be able to turn a blind eye but I'd had to promise there would be no incidents inside the pub for it to be able to continue. He didn't care what happened outside because then it was nothing to do with his pub.
Tom was a little peeved with my response and made his way over to where I stood.

" Did you hear what I said?" he barked in my face. I wasn't in the least bit intimidated by him any more, even less so since I had almost taken him apart in our one and only fight. He had had a grudge ever since and wanted revenge but unknown to me Alice had made him promise not to. I had been waiting for some sort of retribution and couldn't understand why nothing had happened but I was ready for him whenever he wanted, there was so much unfinished business with him.

" How's Alice?" I asked, I was genuinely concerned about her but said it predominantly to annoy him. If he thought I was going to react to his insults then he was going to be disappointed. I'd had a fair couple of days since the incident with the pills and I was still drinking heavily but even though I was still angry about a lot of things I was determined to put a stop to the way I reacted. It would be different if Tom started something but I was getting the impression he was apprehensive about doing so. Mind you if he and Alice weren't together I wouldn't think twice, I was pretty sure I hated him more than he hated me.

" What the fuck's it got to do with you?" was Tom's response and I knew I had already got the upper hand in the situation. He backed off and went to join his mates at the bar.

It looked like he would be in the pub for a while, maybe all night, and I suddenly thought that this might be my one chance to see Alice and the baby.

It was still quite early and I guessed I could make it to the hospital for about seven thirty if I left straight away. I downed the rest of my pint and left by the back door without anyone seeing. As luck would have it a bus was waiting at the stop so I jumped aboard and paid my fare. Within half an hour I was walking towards the hospital entrance and once inside looked at the board in front of me for directions to the maternity ward. It was on the second floor so I made my way up the stairs, turning right at the top to reach the ward reception. I asked the nurse behind the desk where Alice was, lying to her that I was her brother before being shown to the bed that Alice was lying on. She had her eyes closed but as I pulled up a chair to sit beside her they flicked open.

" Hi," I said, " how are you feeling?"

I'm sure she was surprised to see me but she greeted me like an old friend and that put me at ease. I had come to see the baby but that seemed a secondary thought now that I'd seen Alice. She looked tired but it didn't distract from her beauty and all the problems I'd had in my mind for the past six months just seemed to float away as if they hadn't even existed. We chatted for a few minutes then I got up to have a look in the hospital cot that was on the other side of the bed.

PUTTING IT RIGHT

I instantly knew that there was no way I could be the father of Alice's child for it was, even at such an early age, the spitting image of Tom.

" Have you seen Tom?" Alice inquired of me. I was tempted to lie and say no but I told her the truth.

" Yes, he was in the George about an hour ago, he even tried to have a go at me."

I heard Alice sigh and noted the unhappy expression on her face.

" He hasn't even been to see us yet, you're the first one. I've been alone for nearly four hours."

I felt sorry for her but really she knew what to expect, Tom thought of nothing but himself.

" He's drinking," I told her, " I doubt if he'll be in tonight. At least I still care enough to be here." I was being sarcastic intentionally.

" I'm sorry Roo, but you know I had to stay with Tom. I couldn't get rid of it and how would you have felt bringing up another man's child?"

I didn't know if it was a question or a statement, was she offering me another chance to be with her and the baby. If she was then I knew the answer. I had come to the hospital with the faintest of hopes that Alice's child was mine but now I was sure it wasn't there was no way that I could stay around watching it grow up. As much as I would miss Alice it was time to leave. I had to start a new life elsewhere.

I told Alice of my plans even though I had only just thought of them, it was early April and I thought I could get seasonal work at some coastal resort anywhere in the country it didn't really matter. I wouldn't be in again to see Alice just in case Tom was there so this might be the last time I ever saw her.

" I've got to go now," I said and took her hand in mine, " no matter what Alice I will always love you, take care and be happy."

I kissed her gently on the lips, turned round and left. I didn't hear her whisper,

" And I'll always love you too."

I'd had my last drink in the George, I walked straight past after I got off the bus that took me home. I made my peace with my parents and told them of my plans saying that it was the only way I felt I could deal with my problems by making a fresh start.

I picked up the newspaper the next morning and hurried through the pages to reach the situations vacant. There were a couple of live-in positions in hotels but one job caught my eye, a holiday camp was looking for all types of staff for help through the summer season. Perfect, loads of people having fun it was just what I needed. I gave them a call and after giving them details of my experience they offered me a job there and then and could I start in a week's time. For the first time in ages I was ecstatic. Things were looking up.

CHAPTER SEVENTEEN

Turning my back on everything was the single most difficult thing I had ever had to do. Leaving behind everyone I had come to love was especially traumatic but deep down I knew it had to be the turning point of my life. Despite losing Alice I realised she had taught me so much and it was because of her that I felt confident enough to move on. I didn't want to leave her behind because I didn't trust Tom but it was impossible for me to stay.

I knew the first few months would be emotionally hard as I had never ventured away from home alone before and despite reassuring my parents that I would be back soon I had no intention of visiting for a long time. Obviously I was going to keep in touch as often as possible by letter and phone but I'd decided to immerse myself in work until such time I considered myself a success and it was only then that I felt I would be able to hold my head up high in my home town. Hopefully by then the few people that were responsible for causing so much pain in my life would no longer be around.

PUTTING IT RIGHT

I didn't see Alice again before I left for my new job. She had come out of hospital and returned to her parents with baby Dean. I heard that she wasn't moving in with Tom until he asked her to marry him but whether that was true or just a rumour I couldn't say. I'd assumed that one day they would get married but it wasn't a subject I wished to dwell on.

I borrowed a suitcase from Mum and packed it with enough clothes and essential things that I would need for at least the first two weeks. I was certain that by then I would be acclimatised to the campsite and would be able to fend for myself.

I had arranged for a taxi to take me to the train station and I was busy saying my goodbyes to Mum and Dad when it pulled up outside the house. Just by being there Dad was showing how much he cared about me as he had taken a day off work without pay. Mum was over emotional and I was trying hard not to let it affect me but I had a lump in my throat and a tear in my eye.

I didn't keep the taxi driver waiting long, Dad followed me to the gate where he shook my hand, thrusting some money he could ill afford into my coat pocket. I didn't want to take it but knew Dad would see it as an insult if I didn't.

Mum stayed indoors, she said she couldn't bear to see me leave, just saying goodbye, she said, was bad enough.

I climbed into the taxi as Dad wished me all the luck in the world,

" Goodbye son." he called as the car pulled away with me waving through the open window.

I brushed away my tears and sat back in my seat gazing out of the window. We drove out of the estate and past the playground, the George and the precinct. I was saying goodbye to my own small world and hoping that I would be saying hello to a bigger and better one.

I was starving when I arrived at the station, I had been too nervous to eat breakfast so I grabbed a sandwich at the platform buffet and ate it while I waited for my train to arrive. I was glad that I didn't have to change trains anywhere along the route because I was sure I would manage to get lost. Apparently somebody was to meet me when I arrived at the resort station to take me to the campsite and I was grateful for that as it meant I would know somebody before I got there.

The journey took about three hours and I hated every minute of it. I'd never been on a train before and the bouncing motion of the carriage made me feel quite queasy. I was glad that I had eaten the sandwich otherwise I think I would have been sick. I finally arrived at my destination and got off the train dragging my case behind me. As it turned out there were three of us waiting for a lift to our new place of work. We all introduced ourselves and I knew at that moment I wasn't going to be homesick or lonely.

We were shown to our sleeping quarters when we arrived at the site. I was to be sharing a chalet with two others, both male. One was a first timer like me but the other had been coming for the past three years. He took us under his wing and told us that if we could cope with the long hours then we would have the time of our lives. He wasn't wrong, although I had to work seven days a week, splitting my shifts between mornings and nights, I had the best seven months of my life.

I began, because of my experience, in one of the restaurants. I was happy when I was told what I would be doing but when I reported for duty the following day I found out that I was waiting on tables, taking orders from customers and clearing the mess they left behind. It was hard work but it made the time go very quickly.

I must have made a reasonable impression the first couple of weeks because one day I was asked to work in the kitchen. This I was told was because somebody liked me, I just thought it was because they were short staffed. However I was asked a few more times over the next week and I was beginning to think that maybe someone really did like me.

I never had any problems with any other staff members, we were just one big happy family and it was nothing like the life I had left behind. The fear that it would be emotionally hard for me never materialised and I was fast becoming the person I'd always wanted to be. I was actually becoming popular, not only with the girls as I'd always been but also with all the other men too. I still thought of Alice especially when I lay in my bed at night and hoped that everything was well with her and the baby, but as much as I wished I could talk to her, because I missed her terribly, I realised we both had different lives.

I phoned Mum and Dad more regularly than I thought I would but I never mentioned Alice and neither did they. They were relieved I sounded so happy but Mum still managed to cry when the time came to put the phone down.

By the end of the season I was so settled I didn't want to leave, I had progressed to a permanent job in the kitchen and was so full of confidence in myself I had even slept with two of the chalet maids including one on my eighteenth birthday when I showed everybody how to drink. It was a massive party and I invited all my workmates to it, I don't think anybody turned me down, all of them popping in for a drink when their shift work allowed. I organised the party when I was having an off day as my birthday approached, thinking that getting drunk would help to take away the recurring pain and it was a big success, I was so busy running around during the day that I didn't stop once to think about what Tom had done to me two years previously. We didn't stop until four in the morning when the last half dozen went back to their own chalets leaving me alone with a local girl called Tania. The sex wasn't particularly memorable but it was satisfying none the less, I knew it wouldn't happen again so I didn't go out of my way to please her just taking advantage of her inebriated state and doing things I'd never done before.

I was asked if I wanted to be considered for the following season and there was only one answer I could give. That left me with a small problem, what to do whilst waiting for the new season to start. I had four months to wait and there was no way that I was going to go back home. A couple of the others had decided to stay as well and had rented a flat locally, getting casual work from one of the hotels that had a year round trade to pay for it. I asked if I could join them and they were happy to let me do just that.

I called home and told my parents that I wouldn't be back to see them over the Christmas holiday because of my new job at the hotel, they were devastated as they hadn't seen me for so long and I sensed a rift was developing between us. I had managed to save a fair amount of money and offered them the chance to spend the festivities at the hotel as my guests but they turned me down. This saddened me but I wasn't surprised.

Over the next few months my calls home became infrequent and even when I did phone, our conversations were short. I tried to blame work commitments but although it didn't help with the hours I worked it wasn't really the truth. I was young and for once I was enjoying life so all I wanted was them to be happy for me. Weekly phone calls became monthly or longer, I knew Dad was angry with me because he didn't come to the phone when I called, he thought I was treating my mother badly by not bothering to visit. I didn't think that was fair because I'd often ask them to come and stay for the weekend in one of the chalets. I think Mum would have stayed but Dad said it was too far away, he was too set in his ways, too much of a home bird and not enough sense of adventure. I wished I had gone home during the winter months but it was too late now that I was back working seven days a week at the site.

Despite the worries that I was losing touch with

my family I didn't let it affect my work and I was still as popular as ever. I had asked if I could get involved with the entertainments side even if it was only once a week but nothing came of it. I wasn't too disappointed as I was still only young but at the end of the season I asked for a meeting with the recruitment manager to see if anything could be done the following year. I came out of the meeting on cloud nine, I had been told that I had been one of many watched all season by the entertainment staff to see if there were any suitable young people that might make the grade. They had been impressed, not only with my attitude to work, but also with my popularity with my colleagues and was I interested in coming back the following year, for a slight increase in salary, as part of the children's entertainment team. I said it was something I wanted so much I would do it for free.

We were allowed to stay in our chalets and use the sites facilities for two weeks after the last of the holidaymakers had gone home as our end of season bonus. I took time to reflect on the past twelve months. On the good side my birthday had passed without the need to get drunk to forget, it was still a day that bothered me greatly but with the passing of time and the fact that my life was progressing forward so rapidly all the pain of the past was becoming a distant memory. I wondered briefly what sort of state I would be in if I had stayed at home.

On the downside however, my relationship with Mum and Dad had deteriorated to the point of virtually no contact and I knew that I wouldn't be going home for Christmas. I wished I could tell them the real reasons I didn't want to go back home but it would have been impossible even to tell a complete stranger meaning it would have to remain a secret for the rest of my life. I hadn't spoken to Dad for over nine months and any phone call I did make was usually in the mornings when I knew he wouldn't be there.

I spent the close season as I had done the previous year only this time I made the renting of the flat permanent. I was planning on staying in the area for a long time and wanted something better than the live-in quarters at the campsite. It was going to cost a lot more money because the chalet was rent-free but at least I had a place to call home.

I was due to restart work in the middle of March, a month before we opened to paying guests. It was basically to plan our programme of entertainment and rehearse so that we all knew what we were supposed to do come the opening of the site. I came up with lots of ideas and was thrilled when a couple of them were implemented. I hadn't worked with children before and was a little bit wary of what I was letting myself in for, but as with the previous two years my trepidation was unwarranted and I took to it like a duck to water. I felt I was born to entertain and remembered back fleetingly to something Alice once said when I was larking about,

" You're so funny you should be a comedian."

Maybe it was a prophecy, she had seen something in me that I didn't know existed. I found myself wishing she was with me, she would have been so proud. I thought about asking Mum if she knew how Alice was but then imagined her to be married with even more children and decided that I would be better off not knowing.

Time was passing by so fast and the summer seasons came and went. Over the next few years I had progressed from entertaining small children to teenagers and finally the hardest job of all, keeping the adults amused.

I had begun to get more time off and was only working five out of seven days and it was because of that I was able to repair the damaged relationship that I had with Mum and Dad. I was financially pretty well off and able to move into my own house and I think that it was because of that that I was able to convince Mum and Dad to come and stay. It had been six years since I had last seen them and even though I felt so guilty I had no one to blame but myself.

The weekend they stayed I was so fraught I think I must have said sorry to them both about a thousand times and still wasn't convinced they had accepted. They asked me if I would come home that year for Christmas but I turned them down, I wasn't ready to face the ghosts of my past. However when I returned the invitation and asked them to stay with me, surprisingly they accepted.

Christmas that year was probably the best ever, Mum and Dad stayed a whole week and I went out of my way to make their stay memorable. Dad really surprised me and took to the seaside town like he'd lived there all his life.

" I've always wanted to retire to the coast." he enthused on many occasions. Mum just looked at me and rolled her eyes, it was something she hadn't heard about. I was so pleased the family was back together again and so ashamed of the stubbornness I'd shown in the past.

They came to stay with me a lot after that, even during the summer when I was working. I'd managed to reach as far as I could go at the campsite and was performing my own one-man show on Friday and Saturday nights. I had been approached to do an audition for a television talent show but I was a bit unsure about my abilities and turned them down. Mum and Dad told me I was stupid and kept saying they couldn't believe how talented I was and that I might not get another chance. I wasn't too bothered, I was still only twenty-three years old and was the happiest I had ever been. I didn't need my life to take on another direction, at least not then. I was still ambitious enough to want it in the future but there was a nagging doubt in my mind that I wouldn't be able to deal with any setbacks. I'd met enough people over the past six years who had 'nearly made it' and ended up where I was starting from. If I was going to be successful long term then I had to take it slowly and listen to the experiences of others.

CHAPTER EIGHTEEN

I'd been away from home for sixteen years when I received the phone call from my father, he was absolutely distraught and I instantly knew it was about Mum. I managed to calm him down enough for him to be able to talk to me sensibly and found out that Mum was terminally ill with cancer. She had less than six months to live. I was devastated and for the first time in years I cried. Mum and Dad had both known for a while that she was ill but had kept it from me, Dad said it was because they hadn't known for definite and that it would have only worried me. I felt helpless, I was so far away from home and I wanted to be with Mum. I knew it was time to go home.

I had become quite well known in my local area, a bit of a celebrity, and I had moved on from the holiday camp. I still performed there as a star guest once a month but mostly I toured the area playing at pubs and clubs with my one man show. It had all come about when I had another offer to audition, this time I went and did well. I appeared on the New Talent T.V. Show and although I didn't win, it certainly got me noticed. Offers kept coming in so I decided to go self-employed. My bosses at the campsite were pleased but disappointed that I would be leaving so I promised that I would perform there whenever I could. The camp was my best friend and I couldn't just walk away.

Being self-employed meant I could do what I wanted to do and that meant being with Mum. I had a couple of commitments that I couldn't get out of but I reassured Dad that I would be home within the week.

It was a strangely uncomfortable feeling that I had when I returned home. From the moment that I stepped off the train onto the station platform I felt I was seventeen again, it was like being in a time warp. Everything I had managed to forget about had become real again, it felt more stomach churning than a first night concert and I'd had a few of those.

I made my way to the taxi rank and got into one at the front of the queue giving the driver the address of where I wanted to go. I sat back as the car started and then drove off. As we got closer to my old home I felt my heart rate intensify and the hairs on the back of my neck began to rise. As much as I didn't want reminding of my past I was hoping that I might spot Alice and I imagined myself as some sort of hero returning to win back the girl of his dreams. But as with most fantasies my hopes were dashed, I didn't spot Alice or anyone else I knew. Sixteen years was a long time and although the place still looked the same I realised that eventually everybody moves on.

We drove past the George and on towards the playground, I looked in as we passed. A few children were playing on the same swings and roundabout that I used to play on. I smiled at the apparent normality of everything and thought that maybe returning home was not going to be as dreadful as I'd feared.

I stood with my suitcases by my side as I knocked on the door of my childhood home. I no longer had a key and I felt like a stranger, a door-to-door salesman carrying his wares in his bags hoping to sell enough of his company's products to keep himself in a job the following week.

I hadn't given an exact time for when I would be arriving, train delays made that impossible, and I'd asked Dad to keep it a secret from Mum so that she wouldn't be spending all day watching through the curtains. Dad opened the door and I went inside, shaking his hand and giving him a hug. He looked tired and I felt sorry for him but I was there now and could take some of the pressure away from him.

I couldn't believe how Mum looked when I

entered the front room, she had stayed at my house less than ten weeks ago and I didn't think anyone could deteriorate as rapidly as she had seemed to do. I burst into tears and we hugged where she sat in her chair. I didn't want to see her like that; I didn't want her to die.

Mum appeared remarkably strong mentally about her illness, she had recognised that her death was inevitable and we spent the next few hours talking non stop. A lot of the time we reminisced about the past, I tried to talk about the future but Mum always changed the subject, it was as though the future didn't exist and for her I had to accept that there wasn't much of it left. She wanted, she said, to die happy and the only way she could do that was to remember all the good times in her life. I cried a lot but Mum took the pain away by making me laugh, I hadn't really noticed before just what a comical person she was and I thought maybe that was where I got my sense of fun from and I would always be in her debt.

I was a little downcast later on in the evening, Mum had gone to sleep in her chair, she was sleeping downstairs as she was too weak to climb the stairs, and looking at her propped up on her pillows was heartbreaking. Dad tried to cheer me up by saying that she hadn't had a day that good for at least two weeks but it had little effect as it

only meant that I was going to see her a lot worse.
I sent Dad off to bed early because he was desperately tired and I sat up with Mum all night. It was my first night back and I didn't want to leave her alone. She woke a few times and I heard her crying quietly to herself, I knew then that she hadn't really come to terms with what was happening to her. I tried to get some sleep as best I could with my head resting on the arm of her chair and my hand clutching hers as tightly as I dared.

I spent the next day running around doing all the things that Dad hadn't managed to do, cleaning the house, washing clothes and a little shopping. I told Dad that if he wanted a break then maybe he should go to work even if it was just to visit. They had been so supportive, giving him as much time off as he needed but he wouldn't leave Mum for a second. He said it was his duty as a husband to be there at the end and he wouldn't have been able to forgive himself if he wasn't. I admired his dedication to her and knew that he truly loved her but I was worried about how he would react to life without her.

Mum was really bubbly during the next few days but it concealed the fact that her life was slowly ebbing away. When she thought no one was looking I could see the pain etched on her face and I had to leave the room, I no longer wanted to cry in front of her.

CHAPTER NINETEEN

The atmosphere at home was getting a bit claustrophobic and Dad could see I was struggling to cope with the prospect of losing Mum. I had been there for a week and had only been out of the house twice to do some shopping. Diplomatically he suggested I should go out one evening so that he could spend some time alone with Mum, he said he had things he wanted to say to her that he couldn't while I was around. I assumed he meant that he wanted to say goodbye.

I took him up on his offer and that evening I went into town. I had thought about going into the George on previous days but always chose not to just in case Tom or any of his mates still drank in there. I wasn't in any fit state emotionally to put up with any trouble from him.

I phoned to book a taxi in the afternoon and spent the rest of the day tidying up my appearance leaving home around eight and telling Dad I wouldn't be late back. I wasn't really in the mood for drinking or even enjoying myself so I'd decided just to have a couple and then head home. The taxi arrived and I asked the driver where the best place in town was for a quiet drink. He mentioned a few places and dropped me off outside one of them saying that it was somewhere people of my age usually went. I entered the pub and ordered a pint of lager at the bar. I hadn't drunk much over the previous five years because of my career, it didn't do to take to the stage having had one too many, even after performing I didn't usually exceed two pints. I lifted the glass to my lips and took a mouthful, it tasted good and the rest of the pint soon followed. Catching the eye of the barmaid I bought myself another drink and swiftly downed that too.

" Steady on!" she said, smiling as she handed me the change from my third pint. I was about to tell her to mind her own business but seeing her smile so genuinely I realised she was only being friendly. We struck up a conversation mainly about the unfairness of life and I carried on drinking. I began to feel quite good and put it down to the company I was with and not the amount of alcohol I was consuming. Even though I hadn't planned to stay out late I remained in the bar until closing time. Mary, the barmaid, was busy wiping down the tables when I approached her and asked if she fancied going on to a club when she finished.

" I'm sorry," she replied, " but I've got to get

home."

" I just knew you wouldn't be on your own, he's a lucky man." I told her before asking, " Are there any decent clubs around here?"

Mary gave me directions to one she knew.

" It's only been open a short while but it seems quite popular, have a good time."

I was impressed by her nature and the hope that I would see her again crossed my mind as I made my way towards the club she had told me about.

I found it quite easily and went inside, climbing the stairs and paying my entrance fee to the girl sitting at the reception desk. The noise of the club hit me as I pushed through the double swing doors that led to the bar and dance floor. I estimated that there were about two hundred people in the club all of whom seemed to be enjoying themselves. I sat down on a vacant barstool and waited to be served. As I was feeling bloated from all the lager I requested a large whisky with ice, which was duly fetched, and I turned on my stool to face out across the dance floor as I drank.

A couple of times I was approached by girls asking to dance but even though I would normally accept I had to say no. If I had tried moving energetically after the amount of alcohol I'd had I would have fallen flat on my face.

I stayed where I was and continued to drink steadily until I heard the D.J. call last orders whilst playing the obligatory slow numbers. I was just getting up to leave when I felt a tap on my shoulder from behind the bar. I looked around and came face to face with somebody I didn't recognise.

" Hello." he beamed before enthusiastically thrusting out his hand towards me.

" Do I know you?" I said puzzled, my words slurring as I spoke.

" Nick Mulvey, owner of this club," he explained, " and you are, if I'm not mistaken, the one and only Roo Reynolds."

His hand was still waiting for my response so I shook it, amazed that he knew who I was.

" Do you fancy another drink?" Mulvey inquired.

" Well," I hesitated, " I was just leaving and you've called last orders."

" Oh don't worry about that," his voice boomed out, " it'll be on the house, I'll just get rid of the crowd and come and join you."

I was so intrigued, I had to stay.

The music stopped and the lights flicked on, a few stragglers finishing off their drinks were shown the door by the bouncers and the once bustling club was quiet.

" So what you drinking then?"

Mulvey was back holding two glasses.

" Scotch?"

" Yeah, that sounds good." I replied.

" You must be wondering who the hell I am?" Mulvey called over his shoulder as he filled the glasses from the optics. Not waiting for a reply he instructed one of his barmen to bring a bottle of whisky over to a table, nodding me in the direction of it as he placed one of the glasses in front of me.

" Over there, I'll join you in a second."

It sounded like an order but I'm sure he didn't mean it as such. His manner was so infectious, affable even and on first impressions I quite liked the guy. I did what he requested and sat down at the table.

" Cheers." he said as he held up his glass towards mine when he finally joined me. We clicked our drinks together and raised them to our lips swallowing the fluid simultaneously. I didn't take my eyes off him as I drank and watched as he slammed his glass onto the table once he'd finished.

" John!" he bellowed, just as the young barman came from behind the bar carrying a bottle of whisky.

" Sorry boss." he apologised as he set the bottle

down on the table in front of us. Mulvey unscrewed the cap and poured us both another glassful. I was really not in a fit state to drink any more and thought that if he wanted to talk then he'd better hurry up before I passed out.

" This is brilliant," he said after emptying his glass for the second time, " getting to meet Roo Reynolds... in my club."

I was confused to say the least, he obviously thought he knew me from somewhere so I asked him to explain. It turned out that he had holidayed at the camp I worked at every year for about ten years. Apparently I had given him and his family so much fun and laughter that they couldn't wait to return every summer just to see me. It hadn't occurred to me until that moment that the people who had stayed on the site actually came from all over the country and that I was probably better known than I thought. It was quite a scary observation to have made and I felt that the privacy that I needed whilst being with Mum would be threatened. I wanted to go home but I'd drunk so much I didn't fancy looking for a taxi. Mulvey wouldn't stop talking about me and the past but did so in such a friendly way that I couldn't get up to leave for fear of being seen to be rude. We carried on drinking and chatting, I told him about Mum's illness and he was genuinely concerned.

" Anytime you need to escape," he said, " you'll always be welcome here."

I knew that I would take him up on his offer one day because the night had been good for me and I felt that Mulvey and I could become firm friends.

My head was thumping when I awoke and it took me a few moments to ascertain where I was. The empty scotch bottle on the table in front of me served to rectify my disorientated mind. I had drunk so much during the night I must have passed out where I sat. Mulvey was nowhere to be seen and I imagined he had disappeared to a bed amused by the fact that he had out-drunk me. My throat was parched and I needed a drink so I got up and went to the bar. I saw a sink at the far end and as I made my way towards it I took a clean glass down from a shelf before pouring myself some water.

Discarding the tumbler into the sink when I finished I looked around the club for signs of life. It was quiet and I wondered how I was going to get out, it was nine thirty in the morning and I needed to get home. In one corner I spied a door marked PRIVATE so I walked over with the intention of going through to find out where it led but just as I got there it burst open and in came the effervescent Mulvey clutching two mugs of steaming coffee.

" Thought you could do with this." he said, offering me one of the mugs, I took it gratefully. There was no need to ask him how he was feeling because he looked like he hadn't had a drink for weeks. Mulvey looked at me and burst out laughing.

" You drink too much," he said, " next time can you pay for it?"

I smiled at his humour, it was something I had needed. For all my abilities at making other people laugh this was a time in my life when I needed someone to do the same for me. I had been getting so despondent with the atmosphere at home that meeting Mulvey had been a great release for all the frustration I had been feeling. I wanted to stay and get to know Mulvey better but it was more important to get home. Dad wouldn't have worried but I ought to have gone back instead of being out all night, anything could have happened to Mum. I asked Mulvey if I could use the telephone and give Dad a call and was relieved as I heard the news that Mum had had a settled night and had gone to sleep smiling. I remembered that he had said he had things to say to her in private and was glad that in the event of her inevitable death she would go knowing just how much she was loved. I knew I had to face up to saying goodbye to her soon before her condition worsened to the extent that she didn't know who I was. It was going to be hard not just saying goodbye but finding the right words to use. I said farewell to Mulvey so that I could go and find myself a taxi but he offered to drive me home himself. His incredible persona meant it would be impossible to turn him down so I accepted and after a few minutes we were making our way outside towards his car.

" I can't wait to tell Sami about meeting you." he said before telling me all about his girlfriend.

" You've just got to meet her, come to the club anytime and we'll arrange a meal or something." he unintentionally ordered as we pulled up outside my parent's house.

" I will." was all I managed to reply. The car door barely had time to close behind me as Mulvey sped off down the road.

CHAPTER TWENTY

Dad was in good spirits when we greeted each other, he made fun of my dishevelled appearance saying I'd better not let my mother see me like it. Obviously he was only joking so I ignored him and opened the door to the front room. Mum was sitting up in her chair reading, something I hadn't seen her do since I had returned home. She looked towards me as I entered lowering the magazine to rest against her lap.

" You look like you had a good night!" she said turning her head upwards as I gave her a kiss on the cheek.

" Yeah, not bad," I replied, " Dad said you had a pretty good night too."

She looked at me intently and grasped my hand with all the strength she could muster.

" He made me feel like a teenager again," she started, her voice was trembling and I could feel her decimated body begin to shake, " will you promise me you'll look after him?"

" Oh Mum, of course I will, you know that."

I noticed tears had begun to form in the corners of her eyes so I reached into the top pocket of my jacket and pulled out a handkerchief. It smelt a bit smoky from being in the club but I still offered it to her. She took it from my hand and dabbed away the moisture telling herself not to be so silly.

" I promised your father there would be no more tears."

I tried to lighten the mood as best I could and we talked for a while, mainly about my night out until Dad came in with a tray of tea. Mum had been struggling with food and one of the small pleasures she had left was dunking biscuits. She always had two cups of tea, one for drinking and one for dunking.

" Oh bugger it!" she would say as her reactions had slowed somewhat and she lost more biscuits to her dunking cup than she managed to get into her mouth. Eventually I left the ensuing comical scene behind and went upstairs to clean myself up.

I had a surprise later on in the evening, Mum, Dad and I were relaxing in front of the television enjoying each others company when there was a knock on the door and to my astonishment standing on the step when I opened the door was Mulvey clutching a bunch of flowers.

" Hi," he said pointing to the flowers, " I hope you don't mind but these are for your mother."

To say I was shocked was an understatement; I

couldn't believe that someone I hardly knew could do something as thoughtful as that. I mumbled my appreciation and invited him inside so that he could present the bouquet to my mother himself. Mum was, to say the least, understandably overwhelmed.

" Get a vase, get them in water." she ordered my father who took them from her and disappeared into the kitchen.

I offered Mulvey a drink.

" Everything except alcohol," I revealed, " we never have any in the house."

Mulvey looked surprised, I guessed the impression I'd left him with at his club didn't make much sense, he probably thought that it would be here if anywhere he could guarantee himself a shot of whisky.

" Coffee will be fine," he finally decided and I ventured into the kitchen where Dad was busy arranging the flowers.

Mulvey stayed for hours talking non stop, it didn't seem to bother him that for the most part it was just a one way conversation but that was his way and I couldn't dislike him for it.

At about eleven o'clock he got up to leave bidding farewell to Mum and Dad. I showed him to the door and thanked him again on behalf of Mum for the flowers.

" Tuesday, dinner...you, Sami and me" he said as he left giving me the name of the restaurant and time to be there. It was as though he had just decided on the spur of the moment and I didn't have a chance to say no.

Tuesday came around quickly and I felt a little nervous as the time came to leave. I hadn't spoken with Mulvey since his visit although I had toyed with the idea of giving him a call to meet for a drink only deciding against it in the end so that I could spend time with Mum. Both Mum and Dad had been impressed with the friendliness of the man and they said they could see us becoming great friends. Mum was especially pleased as she saw it as a sign that I would stick around after her time had come.

" Maybe you could find a nice girl too and move back here to live."

Her words embarrassed me slightly, I hadn't had a serious relationship to speak of since the time I was seeing Alice. I'd slept with lots of girls, mainly one night stands during summer seasons at work and one had even lasted two months but in my heart there was no one who could ever replace the feelings I had for Alice. I compared every girl I ever met to Alice and none of them ever came close, I didn't think I could ever say 'I love you' to anyone ever again.

PUTTING IT RIGHT

I sighed deeply at the memories of my lost love and for a moment thought I really should try to find her, but what purpose would it have served, she might even be blissfully happy with Tom but I doubted it.

I said goodbye to my parents giving them the name of the restaurant I was dining at just in case. It was only the second night I'd been out in the time I'd been back and as I clambered out of the taxi when it reached town I decided on a quick drink before I met up with Mulvey and Sami.

I went into the pub where I'd met Mary hoping that she was working but I was disappointed to find out that she wasn't. I sat at the bar drinking hoping that she still might walk in but by the time I left she hadn't.

The restaurant, Mulvey informed me, was two doors down the road from his club and I slowly made my way to it. I presumed he would have made the reservation in his name and told the waiter so when he greeted me. I had arrived ten minutes late in the hope that Mulvey and his girlfriend would already be there but as it was I was still first to arrive. I always felt awkward waiting alone in a restaurant, I felt that people were staring at me which considering what I did for a job was a little hard to fathom. I went to the bar and ordered a drink, unusually for me I chose a glass of wine and I stayed there while I waited.

It was twenty minutes after I had arrived and whilst I was ordering my third glass of wine that Mulvey and Sami came through the door.

" Sorry we're late," Mulvey apologised rather loudly, " but Sami couldn't find a thing to wear."

" What are you drinking?"

My question was to both of them but directed at Sami because I couldn't take my eyes off her, she was absolutely stunning wearing the tightest, shortest, and most low cut black dress I had ever seen.

" Alright, put your eyes back in your head," Mulvey laughed, " she's spoken for."

" A large vodka and tonic, tall glass, ice no lemon." Sami answered my question and I redirected her request to the barman.

" And we'll take a bottle of your house red please, Gianni." Mulvey asked the same barman after spotting my half drunk glass.

The waiter appeared and told Mulvey that his table was ready if we would like to make our way through to the dining area. I noted that Mulvey seemed to be on first name terms with all the staff and guessed that he was a regular patron a fact that was confirmed when he made his order without looking at the menu.

" Lobster Thermidor for me and Sami, thank

you Luca."

" I'll have the peppered steak, medium rare please." I said to Luca after looking through the menu. It was the prices that made me choose the steak, I didn't think I had ever been in a more expensive place and I hoped I hadn't offended Mulvey by taking the cheaper option.

Mulvey poured the wine as we sat waiting for our food and as on the two previous occasions I'd spent in his company he did most of the talking. He was infatuated with Sami and he reminded me of the way I felt about Alice but I wasn't convinced that Sami felt the same way about him. There was something disconcerting about her for all her obvious beauty.

The meal was served and devoured with relish, it was quite simply the best I'd tasted in a long time and I thought well worth the money. Mulvey and I went through two bottles of wine while Sami stuck to her vodkas, quite a few of them.

" Choose yourself a sweet," Mulvey said, getting to his feet and handing me another menu, " I'm off to the gents."

I glanced through the menu looking at all the exotic sounding sweets on offer and was about to pass it to Sami when I felt her hand on my thigh rather nearer to my groin than I was comfortable with. I moved back in my chair and looked at her in surprise.

" You can take me out one night, if you want." she said as she withdrew her hand but not before giving my groin a playful squeeze.

" I'm sorry?" I stammered, and I'm sure I blushed for the first time since my teens. I was shocked and didn't know what else to say. I had felt unsure about Sami but I wasn't expecting her to make a play for me, especially as Mulvey wasn't far away.

" No," I said when I had regained a bit of composure, " Nick's my friend."

" I could be a better one!"

Sami's words were so brazen I knew she meant it but there was no way I could do that to a friend whether I fancied Sami or not. Seeing Alice behind Tom's back was different because I loved Alice and hated Tom. I was beginning to dislike Sami and felt sorry for Mulvey. How could she repay his obvious love for her by behaving like that.

We were sitting in silence when Mulvey returned but I don't think he noticed any friction between us. I couldn't stay any longer I felt so uncomfortable so I made my excuses about having eaten too much and the need to get home to see how Mum was. I asked Gianni to call me a taxi and waited outside until it arrived.

PUTTING IT RIGHT

Mulvey came out of the restaurant to say goodbye
and asked me to come to his club that weekend.
" There's something I need to ask you."

CHAPTER TWENTY-ONE

I had a lot of conflicting thoughts flying around my head over the next few days because of what Sami had asked me to do. Unknown to me she had slipped a card with her phone number on it into my jacket pocket. I was tempted to call her to tell her exactly what I thought of her but decided it better to just leave her alone. I hoped I wouldn't have to meet her again too soon especially Saturday night when I had arranged to meet Mulvey at his club. I wanted to tell Mulvey what Sami had said to me but it was none of my business, maybe he knew what she was like, maybe he was he same, I didn't know I'd only known him a couple of weeks but I didn't really know a thing about him. It felt like I was going over everything that had happened with Alice and me again but from a different viewpoint, I was on the outside this time looking in. I didn't want my mind to get as screwed up as it had before, what was it about this town that seemed to completely fuck me up. I was beginning to wish I hadn't come back.

I phoned Mulvey early on Friday evening hoping

to catch him before he went to open his club. I wasn't thinking too clearly and was a bit surprised when Sami answered. I didn't expect her to be at his flat and I certainly didn't want to talk to her. I tried to be civil but I'm sure I sounded quite rude when I asked her if Mulvey was there. In a way I was glad when she informed me that he had already left because I didn't want to talk to him with the prospect of Sami eavesdropping. I said goodbye to her adding that I'd call him at the club but after putting down the phone decided not to bother. I was going to put off our meeting on Saturday but hearing Sami's voice made me change my mind. For some reason I felt I couldn't let him down.

I went into town at about nine on Saturday night going straight to Mulvey's club. It was busy inside and Mulvey was working behind the bar. He acknowledged my arrival and said he'd join me in a few minutes. I took the lager he had poured me and went to find an empty table, choosing one near the back wall far enough away from the dance floor where it would be easier to talk.

Mulvey joined me after about ten minutes, bringing with him another pint for me. He'd timed it just right as I was pouring the remains of the first one down my throat. We exchanged the normal pleasant greetings and he asked about

Mum who I informed him was pretty much the same as when he had visited.

" So what do you think of Sami?" he asked.

It was a question that I dreaded to answer truthfully so I had to be a bit evasive.

" She's very attractive." I said hoping that would be enough.

" Yeah, I saw you looking. Sorry though Roo, she's mine all mine."

At least that answered one of my fears; he didn't know what she was like behind his back. I still felt he ought to know and was in two minds to tell him there and then, but what if he thought I was only saying it so that I could have Sami all to myself, after all I had just told him that I found her attractive. Damn I told myself, I could never tell him now.

The conversation veered away from Sami and I was glad but then he told me the real reason he wanted to talk to me.

" I would be honoured," he began, " if you would possibly consider appearing here?"

" What do you mean appearing here?" I answered, although I was pretty sure what was coming next.

" Appearing...performing...you know, doing a show for me."

" For you?"

" No, not for me personally, everybody, your fans, you'll get paid and I'll earn a bit too."
I had my doubts; it wasn't anything that had even crossed my mind. I was back home because of Mum and I didn't want anything to detract from that. Plus I didn't want to draw attention to myself especially as I didn't know if Tom or Alice were still in the area, it would only be stirring up trouble, trouble I could do without.

" I don't think I can." I said eventually after giving Mulvey's request some thought. He looked at me with disappointment, he seemed a little hurt.

" At least think about it for a couple of days, I know it's a hard time for you right now but maybe it will help to take your mind off things."
He was doing his best to convince me that it could be a good idea and as I looked at him I saw this friendly kind-hearted man who would probably do anything for anyone given the chance. How could I turn him down, he didn't know about my past and it wouldn't be fair to say no without giving him a true explanation.

" O.K. I'll do it." I finally conceded.
Mulvey was ecstatic and jumped to his feet doing a little jig.

" Let's celebrate!" he shouted and before I could answer ran off to the bar returning seconds later with two glasses and a bottle of scotch. This was getting to be a habit.

We spent the rest of the night drinking and laughing; making plans for my big night as Mulvey called it. I hoped Mulvey would remember what we'd decided because at the rate we were drinking I knew I wouldn't.

Mulvey impressed me with the speed at which he arranged my appearance at his club. He would make a good manager for me if I ever got the need for one I thought. The night was set for the Wednesday of the following week which gave me about ten days to prepare. I agreed with Mulvey that I could pull out at a moments notice depending on the condition of my mother.

I decided to perform the same routine I'd been doing at the camp during the season but then realised I had left all my props and stage clothes there when I had last performed. Mulvey offered to drive me there to get them.

" We'll be there and back in about eight hours," he said.

I took his word for it; I'd only made the journey twice and both times were on the train.

We left at seven the following morning with Mulvey hoping to be back well before five. His club wasn't open that night as it was early in the week so he had planned to take Sami out for the night. She had spent the last few nights at her own flat like she did most weekends as it wasn't very often that Sami actually came to Mulvey's club. She said she hated being in a place like that while Mulvey was working and she would rather spend time on her own or out with some of her girlfriends. Cynically I thought it was just an excuse to be away from Mulvey to do as she pleased.

As it was we were back at four and Mulvey had plenty of time to spare before taking Sami out. We unloaded all my gear at his club before he dropped me back at my parent's house. He popped in briefly in the hope of seeing Mum but unfortunately she had been having a rough day and Dad thought it best if she wasn't disturbed. I was a little bit upset with myself at having been away for such a long time and not even thinking about phoning to see how she was. Looking at her I realised that she hadn't got much time left and apart from doing the night at Mulvey's club I was determined I wasn't going to leave her again.

Mum had been gradually taking increased doses of morphine to try and ease the pain and although it seemed to be doing the job it was meant to I couldn't help thinking that it wasn't enough. I got really angry that night and I couldn't help it but I trashed my bedroom, smashing to bits all my childhood treasures and memories. Collapsing on the floor I cried uncontrollably until Dad came in the room and picked me up.

" I love her Dad." I sobbed into his arms as he hugged me.

" I know son, and so does Mum."

CHAPTER TWENTY-TWO

I desperately needed to pull myself together and I needed to do it quickly. I was no good to Dad if I continued to slide into a state of depression. I needed something positive to focus on and even though it now seemed as if it was a bad idea the forthcoming night at Mulvey's club had to become my escape from the circumstances at home.

I had originally planned to rehearse my set at the club but because of Mum's worsening health and my reluctance to leave her that was no longer possible. I tried to repair the damage I'd caused in my room so I would have somewhere to practice and as I'd done my act so many times I didn't think it would take long to perfect it, providing I could keep my mind clear of negative thoughts.

Mulvey phoned a couple of times to check on the situation, I think he was a little worried that I was going to call the show off but I managed to convince him everything would go ahead as planned.

By Sunday night I felt as though I knew everything off by heart and was glad that it would soon all be over. Mum's condition had stabilised somewhat but occasionally she seemed unable to recognise myself or Dad. It was a sad time and I was so glad that we had both managed to say our goodbyes before Mum's illness had reached such a stage.

I don't really know why but I went through my routine in front of Mum and Dad on Tuesday evening, Dad thought it was very good but Mum hardly knew I was there. Afterwards I called Mulvey to say that it was definitely on. He sounded relieved and told me that all the tickets had been sold and my share would be about a thousand pounds. I replied that I couldn't care less about the money and that I just wanted it all over so that I could get back home to Mum.

I didn't have a particularly good nights sleep, Dad was sitting with Mum because he said he didn't want me tired out before my show but I was awake most of the night listening to Mum crying with the pain. The morphine was having hardly any effect and I began wishing that her agony would soon be all over. It was a horrible thought and I hated myself for it but it would be better if she died quickly.

Mulvey picked me up early on Wednesday afternoon as we had arranged, I had planned a couple of rehearsals and a few drinks to calm the nerves but I didn't have any intentions of staying after my performance and made that clear to Mulvey, insisting that he drove me home immediately afterwards. He promised he would and I had no reason to doubt him.

I went in to kiss Mum goodbye and found Dad busy washing her face, she had been violently sick so I offered to stay and help. Dad would hear none of it and more or less manhandled me out of the house.

" Knock 'em dead son!" he said as I made my way to Mulvey's car.

Despite my reservations, the show was brilliant. It wasn't so much the material I had, it was the audience. They were superb. The warm feeling I got when I walked out on stage was like nothing I had ever felt before. Maybe it was because I was feeling so down about my personal life that made the crowds reaction so uplifting. I completely forgot about everything that was going on at home and became my old self once again.

When I came off stage Mulvey was there waiting to greet me.

" Bloody marvellous." he yelled in my ear as he gave me a great big bear hug before starting to slap me across the back.

" What a wonderful night. Roo, you are a superstar!"

I think he was exaggerating a little bit, I had never

thought of myself as a star let alone a superstar but for once I felt elated. I had missed the buzz of entertaining the past few weeks and was happy to let him drag me off to the bar for a celebratory drink.

Quite a few of the audience had stayed behind for a drink as well and for twenty minutes I was shaking hands and signing autographs. I was amazed, I had truly never known anything like it, I had signed more pieces of paper in one night than I had ever done in a summer season. Either Mulvey was a brilliant salesman of a small-time comedian or I was more popular than I had ever dreamt I could be.

Eventually the attention ceased and I managed to reach the bar with Mulvey where the inevitable bottle of scotch was waiting. Despite my demand to go home straight away it was just what I needed and Mulvey poured me a large glassful. I raised the glass to my lips and took a look around the emptying room. It was then that I noticed someone looking at me, a girl of about eighteen and she was without doubt one of the most beautiful girls I had ever seen in my life. She smiled when she realised she had caught my attention and I sort of smiled back before turning to face Mulvey again. He was talking to me but I wasn't taking any notice, I was more interested in the girl behind me. I looked in her direction again and it was as if she hadn't taken her eyes off me.

" Roo."

I heard my name and felt Mulvey's hand on my shoulder.

" Roo, do you want another drink or do you have to get back home?"

" I'm not sure." I replied rather aimlessly still looking at the girl. Mulvey looked too, trying to make out just what was grabbing my attention.

" Not bad," he said when he caught sight of the girl, " she's a regular at weekends, her name's Jessie."

" You know her?" I questioned Mulvey.

" No, not really, just that she comes here with a few friends on a Friday night. I overheard her name once and you don't forget the name of someone as gorgeous as she is."

" Can you introduce us?" I asked him.

" Do it yourself," he suggested, " you're the star tonight, oh and she drinks lager and black."

I pleaded with Mulvey to go behind the bar and pour me the drink he said she usually drank. He looked at me with a smirk.

" I thought you wanted to go home?"

" I do and I will but just let me buy the girl a drink."

Mulvey hesitated and then sighed as he got off his

stool and vanished behind the bar. He poured what I'd asked for and placed it down in front of me.

" Good luck." he grinned.

I picked up the drink and turned towards the table that Jessie was sitting at. She was still looking at me and I began to feel a little intimidated. This wasn't usually the case when I approached women but there was something about Jessie that made me very nervous. I really wanted to get to know this girl. I started to walk towards her and as I did so she turned her head away. I immediately thought I'd made a big mistake and virtually stopped in my tracks but then she looked at me again and smiled sweetly. I carried on walking in her direction until I'd reached her table managing to stop whatever conversation her friends were having as I said hello. They returned my greeting with varying levels of friendliness and suddenly I felt a bit of a fool. There I was standing in front of four young people each looking at me intently and I was clutching just the one drink. I needed an explanation and had to think quickly.

" Hello," I said again racking my brain trying to work out what to say next, " I wanted to buy you all a drink."

Come on Roo, I thought to myself, you need to do

better than that, why on earth would you want to buy four strangers a drink? I had to stick to my story even though I was uncomfortable with it. I started to mumble desperately searching for the right words.

" My friend Nick Mulvey, the owner of this club said one of you drinks lager and black but he wasn't sure about the rest of you."

Brilliant, I told myself sarcastically, what a way to make an impression, as a total buffoon. All I wanted was to talk to Jessie alone, how was I going to do that now? Then I had an idea.

" Why don't you others go and get what you want and put it on my slate." I said, handing the glass I was carrying to Jessie.

I turned back to face the bar and signalled to the watching Mulvey that I wanted drinks for the others who were already heading towards him.

" Do you always buy drinks for people without asking what they want first?" Jessie queried as I pulled an extra chair up to her table.

" I think it's probably the first time I have ever done it." I replied, feeling a little more relaxed now we were momentarily on our own.

" I couldn't help noticing you looking at me and when Nick mentioned what you usually drank, I had to take the opportunity."

" I'm glad you did, it was a clever way of getting

rid of my friends."

Jessie seemed genuinely impressed even though I hadn't planned it quite like that.

" Thanks," I said modestly, " but before they come back can I ask you a question?"

" Sure, as long as it's not about breakfast!" she said in such a way that I couldn't make out if she was joking or being serious. I hoped she was flirting with me.

" No," I smiled anyway, " I was wondering if you would like to come out one night?"

" I'll be in here on Friday night, ask me then." Jessie answered as her friends returned from the bar.

I was expecting a straight answer not a teasing one. Was she playing hard to get or was she testing me to see if I really was interested? It didn't matter; I knew what I was going to do.

" See you Friday then." I said emphatically as I got up and left them to enjoy the rest of their night. I rejoined Mulvey at the bar.

" You weren't gone long," he said, " turn you down did she?"

" Not exactly." I replied to my friend but he didn't seem to be listening.

" Roo," he started to change the subject, " I want to ask you to do me a really big favour."

" Not another performance?" I begged,

"Tonight was a great night but not again please."

" No, not another night here but a performance just the same. I want you to be my best man. I'm going to ask Sami to marry me!"

CHAPTER TWENTY-THREE

Mulvey's revelation knocked me back, I had returned to the bar a little surprised at Jessie's response to my asking her out and wished I could have stayed talking to her a while longer but her friends had put paid to that. Now, what Mulvey was asking, or rather telling me, had taken all thoughts of Jessie out of my mind.

" You want to marry Sami?"

I didn't mean to but I sounded bewildered and I think it gave the wrong impression to Mulvey. He looked at me more than a little puzzled.

" Yes, don't you think I should?"

What could I say to him, tell him the truth about what I thought of her and what she had asked me? It wasn't up to me; he had to make his own decisions.

" If you really love her."

I was trying to be as sensitive as I could even though I wanted to tell him he was making a big mistake.

" I do, I really do, I love her more than anything." Mulvey said, a big smile returning to his face as if he thought I was giving him my blessing.

" Then you have to ask her."

We had another drink, on Mulvey's insistence, to celebrate his forthcoming proposal. I raised my glass half-heartedly to his future happiness. I looked back towards Jessie and her friends but they had gone and I was annoyed that I had missed seeing her leave. It was time for me to go as well and I told Mulvey that I was off to find a taxi. He wanted to drive me home but I said he had drunk too much and it was better that he didn't. I walked out of the club and into the street half hoping that Jessie might be hanging around but to my horror, getting out of a car a few yards away from the entrance to Mulvey's, I spotted Sami.

" Hi sexy!" she called out when she saw me.

I didn't reply, I was trying to see who was driving the vehicle she was climbing out of but it was too dark and facing the wrong way for me to get a clear view.

" How did the show go?" Sami asked as the car pulled out from the kerb and drove away.

" Very well thanks." I answered her question, not wishing to appear too rude.

" Is Nick still here?"

I replied that he was and then quickly made my excuses to leave as I had to catch a taxi, I didn't want to talk to Sami any longer than I had to but as I made to walk away she stroked the back of her hand down my cheek.

" I meant what I said the other night," she purred, " give me a call."

I couldn't believe her boldness in trying it on again and I realised that I should have made it crystal clear that I wasn't interested in her advances but I hurried away from her without saying a word. My night had been a mixture of highs and lows and I didn't want it to end with thoughts of Sami playing on my mind. I took my frustration out on an empty can lying on the pavement.

" Fucking bitch." I yelled as I chased after the can to give it yet another kick. I wasn't normally prone to such aggressive outbursts but Sami had made me so mad.

" Fucking bitch." I shouted again as the can went bouncing into the road.

" Are you o.k?"

The querying voice came from my right hand side and I looked to see who had spoken, my anger dissipating when I recognised Mary. I gave a dejected sigh and told her that I wasn't, explaining to her the predicament I had found myself in but trying not to mention any names.

" A friends girlfriend is coming on to me and he

thinks she is totally dedicated and faithful to him and I don't know what to do about it."

"You mean you want her?" Mary asked.

" God forbid, not a chance, I mean I don't know if I should tell him or not."

" How good a friend is he?"

" Pretty good, I've only known him a short while but he's always been honest with me. He seems to sort of...hero worship me."

" Do you fancy a coffee?" she trailed off her question and for one moment I thought she was asking me back to her place but then she spoke again.

"There's an all night café just around the corner if you feel like talking."

I was slightly relieved, I didn't want to turn her down because she seemed like a good listener and it might be good to talk to someone about all the things that were starting to screw my head up.

" What time is it?" I enquired and Mary looked at the watch on her wrist before answering.

" Twenty five to midnight."

" Don't you have to be back home, won't your boyfriend be getting worried about you?"

" There isn't one, I live on my own, that is apart from my son but he's nearly sixteen and big enough to look after himself."

" A sixteen year old son!" I was shocked, " You

don't look old enough."

It wasn't meant as a compliment, I thought she was quite attractive but I was genuinely only remarking about her age which I'd only estimated at about twenty five.

" Thanks," she smiled " I had him quite young, now about that coffee."

" O.K. as long as you let me pay for it."

" Too right you will," Mary said, " it's because of you that I'm having it."

I chose a table next to the front window when we reached the café and Mary wandered off to get the drinks. I spied a phone booth in one corner of the room and decided to call home. Dad would still be awake and I wanted to let him know I would be coming home but a little later than I'd planned. He told me that Mum was having a quiet night but I was sure that I could hear her in the background. I felt selfish, what was I doing having a coffee with a relative stranger when I should have been at home with my parents. I suddenly felt depressed again and I must have been looking really miserable when I put the phone down and returned to the table. Mary was waiting with two mugs of steaming coffee.

" What's wrong?" she asked me, " you look so sad."

" Where do I start?" I said forlornly and

slumped down in a chair opposite her.

" Try the beginning." Mary suggested.

" That's probably the worst place."

" Then try somewhere you're comfortable with."

Mary seemed such a nice person; I could put money on her never having had a problem in her life. I thought about telling her about Mum dying but decided that it could wait.

" Do you know who I am?" I asked her. The question sounded a little pretentious but I hoped she hadn't got any idea who I was.

" Well, I've met you once before but I haven't got a clue what your name is, you can tell me if you like."

" It's Roo, short for Rufus."

" That's different, at least it's not common like mine."

" Some sort of family name, I was told why once but I can't remember now."

" Tell me about the girl."

" My friend wants to marry her."

" And you don't think it's a good idea?"

" He loves her."

" But..."

" I told you, she's making it obvious she wants some sort of relationship with me."

" So what do you want to do?"

" I want to tell him, but it'll hurt him, I don't want to break his heart. I know what that feels like."

" So don't do anything."

" But then I'll feel guilty because I don't trust her to be faithful to him."

" Have you seen her with anyone else?"

" No."

" Then you can't judge her and you can't tell him."

In a way Mary was right, I didn't know Sami that well and with no evidence of her cheating I couldn't tell Mulvey she was. I had to let it drop and let him live his life his own way.

" Thanks," I said to Mary, " I don't think I can tell him."

" Mind you, if you are right..." Mary continued with her advice, " just make sure you are there for him to help him through it, everyone needs someone to talk to."

" Don't I know it." I didn't mean to say it as loud as I did but Mary heard my muttering and picked up on it straight away.

" Is there something else bothering you?" she asked, " maybe whoever broke your heart?"

" It was a long time ago."

" Do you want to talk about it?"

" I've never told anyone ever before. It's just

too much of a painful memory."

" I'm sorry," Mary said looking away from me and I noticed she seemed a little on edge, " I'm being too nosey, we've all got secrets we don't want to talk about."

" Even you?"

" I'm sorry I've got to go." Mary was getting anxious, frightened even and she stood up to leave. I didn't understand and tried to get her to sit down again but she wouldn't. I got out of my chair and physically tried to stop her going but she brushed me aside and ran out of the café. I wanted to chase after her but didn't want to cause a scene especially in the street at night so I let her go. I sat down at the table again and finished my coffee mystified at Mary's behaviour. She had given me something else to think about and it was something I had to get to the bottom of. I made up my mind to go to the pub she worked at on Friday before I met up with Jessie.

I ordered another coffee and sat in the corner to drink. I was the only customer, the memory of my performance at Mulvey's earlier had completely vanished, I suddenly felt totally alone.

CHAPTER TWENTY-FOUR

Mulvey called me at home the next day, he wanted me to go into town with him to help choose a ring for Sami. He said he was going to ask her that night after he had cooked her a romantic meal. I didn't feel comfortable about his plans and wanted to tell him to leave me out of it, besides what did I know about Sami's taste in jewellery. Unfortunately Mulvey wasn't a man that anyone could find easy to turn down and it didn't take much persuasion for me to agree.

Dad was exhausted and could have done with a few hours sleep but after I told him what Mulvey had planned he said I couldn't let him down. I promised I would be back as soon as possible to take my turn in looking after Mum.

Thankfully from my point of view we weren't in town very long. Mulvey seemed to think that any ring would do and I wasn't very helpful. He had had the good sense to bring one of Sami's rings with him so he could get the exact size but he was more concerned about how much it was going to cost, I was sure he was thinking that the more he spent on it the more Sami was going to like it. I tried to explain that people's tastes were different and Sami might prefer something that didn't actually cost very much and at the end of the day she was the one that was going to be wearing it. Mulvey took no notice and paid out as much money as he could afford.

" She'll love it," he said as we left the jewellers. He patted the box that was safely concealed in his pocket as he spoke and we made our way back to the car, window-shopping as we went.

" Top hat and tails, I think," Mulvey decided as we passed a gent's outfitters, " sod the expense."

" She hasn't said yes yet." I reminded him.

" She will Roo, I just know it."

Mulvey dropped me off outside my house.

" I'll call you tomorrow," he said, " to let you know how much she loves me."

" You don't need to," I replied, " I'm coming to the club tomorrow night to see Jessie so you can tell me then."

" Maybe, but I want you to be the first to know and I might not be able to keep quiet that long."

" Call me whenever then, I'll be up all night with Mum...it's my turn."

We parted company, Mulvey drove off and I went inside, I wished I hadn't. My blood ran cold at what I saw. The door to the front room was open and I could see the doctor bending over my mother. I feared the worst.

" No...o...o!" I shouted and rushed into the room to find out what was happening.

" It's o.k. She's still alive." I heard Dad but didn't see him until he stepped in between the doctor and myself.

" What's happened, why's the doctor here?"

" I had to call him out, Mum keeps losing consciousness, the ambulance is on its way."
Dad seemed quite calm but I was in a panic, I kept thinking why was I never around when something happened, why was I still being so selfish to keep going out all the time when the only reason I had returned home in the first place was to be with Mum. I virtually pushed the doctor out of the way such was my need to get to Mum.

" Mum," I shouted but looking at the state she was in I doubted that she heard me.

" Mum," I shouted again, hoping for a spark of recognition in her eyes, there wasn't even a flicker, " please don't die, I love you, please don't die."
I felt Dad trying to pull me away as I grabbed hold of her.

" Come on son," I heard him saying, " let the doctor see to her."
I looked at him with tears streaming down my face, why was he being so unemotional, how could

he be so calm and collected, Mum was almost dead and he looked as though he didn't even care. He reached out to give me a comforting hug but I pushed him away and ran from the room out the front door and down the path. I was sitting on the pavement holding my head in my hands when the ambulance arrived and I was still there when Mum was carried out on a stretcher.

Dad and I travelled with Mum in the back of the ambulance barely saying a word to each other until we reached hospital whereupon Dad pulled me to one side as we watched the ambulance men take her stretcher through the emergency doors.

" I've asked if she can be allowed to die naturally." Dad said.

" No, they can save her." I countered but he wasn't listening to me.

" Just plenty of morphine to take away the pain, I don't want her to suffer any more."

He walked away from me following Mum through the entrance so that he could be with her; I went too but kept a distance behind. The doctors that took over from the ambulance men wouldn't let Dad go past reception, instructing him to wait there until they had Mum settled in a bed. Dad just accepted what they told him and made no attempt to follow. He sat himself down on a chair in a small waiting area and picked up a magazine that was lying on a table in front of him. He cut a sad and lonely figure and I understood that his impassiveness was his way of dealing with the inevitable. He couldn't do anything about what was going to happen but he was ready for it and I could no longer be upset with him for that. I went and sat next to him and said sorry. Dad said I had nothing to be sorry about.

Eventually we were told we could go and sit with Mum on the ward and as we walked through the hospital it occurred to me that it was the first time I had been there since Alice had given birth. It was the last memory I had of her and it looked like it was going to be the last memory I would have of Mum too. How ironic it was that the only two women I had loved would both disappear from my life in the same place.

Dad and I stayed with Mum for the rest of the day and all night. I was awake the whole time but Dad would occasionally drift off to sleep in the chair beside Mums bed. She looked quite peaceful lying there but I knew it wouldn't be long before she passed away. I talked to her as much as I could but, not wanting to disturb any other patients, for the most part I just sat there quietly.

Morning came and Dad awoke from another snooze acting a little edgy. I asked him what the matter was and he told me he needed to go home.

" What for?" I asked, slightly puzzled.

" If Mum's going to die then I want her wearing her own clothes not that horrible hospital issue nightgown she's got on now. I want her to have some dignity."

I smiled, if anything was to show me just how much he loved her then that one statement did.

" I'll go," I said even though I didn't want to leave Mum's side, " you've got to be here."

I stayed for another half hour and had a cup of tea from the trolley that was being pushed around by one of the catering staff. I had hoped that Mum would wake before I went but she didn't so I kissed her on the cheek and left her bedside. I hugged Dad firmly before making my way downstairs to the main entrance.

On the wall near the reception desk was a payphone and written on a card next to it was the number of a local taxi firm. I called and asked for a cab to take me home and then went outside to wait.

It turned up within five minutes and I was thankful as it meant that I would be back with Mum and Dad quite quickly. I asked the cabbie to wait when we arrived at the house so that he could take me back to hospital and then disappeared inside to collect Mum's nightclothes.

As I walked through the front door the phone was

ringing and I prayed that it wasn't Dad telling me that Mum had died, it wasn't, it was Mulvey and he sounded distraught. He was talking quickly and loudly and I couldn't understand a word he was saying.

" Nick," I shouted, doing my best to make him hear me, " For God's sake calm down."

" I can't," he shouted back, " it's Sami," he was getting hysterical, " I need to see you, there's been an accident."

" What sort of accident?" I asked but all I heard was a crash, it sounded like Mulvey had dropped the phone and I could hear him moaning in the background.

" Nick." I kept shouting but he didn't pick the phone up again.

" Fuck," I yelled, slamming my own phone down, " I don't need this now."

I dashed upstairs to Mum's room and grabbed a couple of nighties from her draw shoving them into a holdall that I took down from the top of the wardrobe.

" Fuck it!" I yelled again as I ran back downstairs and outside to get in the waiting taxi. I thought I heard the phone ringing again as I went down the path but I chose to ignore it.

Dad knew something was up the moment I arrived back on the hospital ward. I told him about the strange phone call I'd had from Mulvey and he was equally confused.

" I need to get hold of him," I said, " it sounded quite serious."

" Why don't you check with the casualty department," Dad suggested, " that way you don't have to leave the hospital and if it is serious then surely they would know."

It was a good idea and short of going round to Mulvey's club it was the only option I had. I kept thinking though that it wasn't that sort of accident and Mulvey had harmed her himself. I wished I had grabbed the book of telephone numbers we kept on the telephone table as I'd left home, at least that way I could have contacted him. I tried hard to remember his phone number but it was impossible. I wondered if they had a directory at reception, I didn't know his address but that didn't matter, how many Mulvey's would there be in town.

I went to reception first and they let me look through their phonebook. I couldn't believe it, a name I was unfamiliar with before I met him and there were seventeen of them listed, none of them with the initial N. I couldn't spend the next hour on the phone trying to trace him so I handed the book back and asked the receptionist if there had been any serious accidents brought in over the last twenty-four hours. She informed me that the previous night was exceptionally busy; there had been two car accidents, an attempted suicide and an aggravated assault.

" Are you looking for anyone in particular?" I was asked.

" Yes." I said.

" Can you tell me their name?"

That was it, they couldn't help. I realised that I only knew her as Sami; I didn't know anything else about her. Somehow I had to get hold of Mulvey. I asked for the phone directory again and found the number for his club, giving it a call. I knew he wouldn't answer, it was only nine in the morning and neither Mulvey nor his staff started work until mid afternoon. I tried three times just in case I'd got the number wrong when I dialled but it just rang and rang. I thought about going to casualty to see if I could see anything but knew they wouldn't let me in without giving Sami's full name so I left reception and went back upstairs to join Dad.

" Any luck?" he asked me.

" No," I answered, " I don't know where he lives and I don't know Sami's surname so I can't find out if she's here or not."

" Go back home and call him from there." Dad suggested but I had all but given up hope of contacting Mulvey and the thought of traipsing all the way back home for what could be a wasted journey just didn't appeal to me.

" Maybe I'll try and catch him at his club when it opens tonight, it's more important to me that I'm here with you both right now, how is she?" I said looking at Mum, trying to put thoughts of Mulvey out of my mind.

Dad told me the doctors had been round whilst I was downstairs and informed him that Mum probably wouldn't last the whole weekend. They hadn't wanted to give Dad that sort of information but he'd begged them to be honest with him. They were still pumping her full of morphine but in her comatose state it didn't look to me as if they needed to. I couldn't tell any longer whether she was in pain or not.

CHAPTER TWENTY-FIVE

Despite the bustle and activity of the nurses going about their duties, the rest of the day passed by very slowly. I was far too preoccupied with my own thoughts to have much of a conversation with Dad and he spent the day much the same as he had done the night before, drifting off to sleep every hour or so. Mum hardly stirred and we both knew she was clinging to life by a thread.

We took it in turns to wash and freshen up and at lunchtime I wandered off to get a sandwich from the hospital café. It was a warm day and I took it outside to eat, sitting in a quiet garden area normally reserved for recuperating patients. There wasn't anyone else there and I was grateful for the silence, it meant I could think a little more clearly without the background noise of the ward to disturb me.

Everything had been such a rush earlier in the morning and now that things had settled down I could make a few decisions on what to do about Mulvey. He had been a good friend to me and whatever his problem was, I had to help. I remembered the words of Mary telling me I had to be there for him and I made up my mind to try and find him. I was coming to terms with Mum's imminent death and maybe it didn't matter that much if I wasn't around when she actually died. It was different for Dad, he had to be there. I hoped he would understand that I had to go out again that night.

I hadn't forgotten that I was meant to be asking Jessie out later so I knew that I was heading for yet another mixed up emotional night. Hopefully Mulvey's troubles wouldn't be as bad as they had seemed when he called me earlier and I would be able to have enough time alone with Jessie, at least that way the evening would end up on a high note that is unless she turned me down. I didn't think that likely though, there was something about that first meeting that told me she felt the same way I did.

There was something else I needed to do and that was to seek out Mary. Her abrupt departure from the café the other night had been something that was playing on my mind and had to be sorted. I sighed, everywhere I looked there were people with problems and they all seemed to be centralising around me. I couldn't deal with them all in one night so I decided against talking to Mary, she would have to wait.

I finished my sandwich and went back to Dad

telling him that I had decided to try and find Mulvey. He was quite pleased saying that I should try and keep my life as normal as possible instead of hanging around the hospital. I appreciated what he was trying to say but couldn't help thinking when had my life ever been normal.

Dad went to get a bite to eat and I told him to take as long as he wanted knowing full well he would be back within ten minutes. For all his outwardly acceptance to Mum's fate I still knew he was as fucked up inside as I was.

I talked to Mum after Dad left, I didn't know if she could hear me or not but for some strange reason I needed to tell her about Jessie. I'd never talked to either of my parents about any of the women there had ever been in my life and I certainly had never shown any of them off to them. Even when they had come to visit me I had never introduced them to anyone I might have been seeing at the time. Somehow I felt different about Jessie, I could see something in her that made me think that we had some sort of future together and I wanted Mum to know before she died. Maybe if that night went well I could even bring Jessie to meet her.

I stopped talking to Mum as Dad returned, he'd been away for no longer than I had predicted. He asked me what I was talking about but I just replied that it was personal stuff. He didn't pry any further.

I watched my father for the rest of the afternoon trying to imagine what he was thinking. How can you deal with losing the one person you have spent the best part of your life with especially in the way that Mum was going. I kept comparing it with the day I left Alice behind and how I felt about her but that was a decision I was responsible for, Dad had no control over what was happening to him. Even though I was setting my sights on a future with Jessie I knew that Alice would always be my one true love and the memories of her would never be far from my mind. I wished I'd stayed and tried harder to make her mine.

I left the hospital at around six o'clock hugging Dad before I went. I said I wouldn't be back that night but I would phone every hour or so to check on Mum's condition. I promised him that I would be at home from eleven onwards so that if anything did happen he could contact me there.

I phoned Mulvey's flat as soon as I got home but there was no reply and when I called the club John, the barman, just told me he wasn't in yet. He hadn't had any contact with him since the previous evening but expected him in around nine o'clock as usual. I checked my watch and estimated that I would be at Mulvey's about eight which would give me nearly three hours to talk to both him and Jessie. I hadn't arranged a time with Jessie and I hoped she would be in early or at least before Mulvey got there.

I spent the next hour making myself look respectable and got into the taxi when it arrived. I seemed to be getting the same driver every time I called and he joked that he should become my personal chauffeur, I just said that I should have learned to drive.

When we arrived I asked the driver to pick me up again at a quarter to eleven to take me home. I went into the club, the music was already blasting out but there weren't many customers to entertain. I looked around but couldn't see Jessie anywhere so went to the bar and ordered a large scotch. John was serving and I asked him if he had heard from Mulvey but he said he hadn't. I stayed at the bar and waited.

By nine thirty neither Mulvey or Jessie had showed up and I was beginning to think that I'd had a wasted journey. I asked John if he would give Mulvey a call at his flat but when he came back from doing so he said there was no reply.

" Probably on his way in." John told me.

I didn't share his confidence.

I kept watch on the door, looking at all the

newcomers as they entered and finally at ten thirty I saw Jessie appear. She was on her own. I stood up and waved at her as she looked around the bar area. She hurried over when she spotted me and I couldn't help but notice she was a little upset. I wasn't sure but she looked like she had been crying.

Offering my stool to sit on, I asked her what was wrong.

" Can we go somewhere else?" she pleaded with me, "somewhere quiet."

Any thoughts I had of waiting to see if Mulvey would show up vanished and I followed Jessie down the stairs and out of the club.

" I'm sorry," she said, " I wasn't going to come tonight but I knew you would be waiting."

" What's wrong Jessie, you look really shaken, has something happened to you?" I feared the worst, maybe she had been attacked.

" There was a car crash last night, look can we go somewhere else, not here on the street."

I didn't know what to suggest, I had a taxi coming in fifteen minutes but did I dare ask her to come back with me.

" My parents are out all night," I didn't tell her why, " it'll be quiet there."

" Anywhere," she said, " anywhere."

I told her a taxi would be along in a few minutes

and we waited in silence until it turned up. Jessie couldn't stop shaking and I was desperate to find out what was making her so upset. Nothing was said during the ride back home and Jessie was so keen to get inside that she almost ran up the path.

" Hold me Roo." She begged as she stood in the hallway in front of me as I closed the door. I did as I was told, embracing her small frame with my arms. She was so vulnerable and I needed to know what it was that I seemed to be protecting her from.

" Do you want to talk about it?" I finally asked when the warmth of my body had gone a long way to rectifying her shaking.

" Yes." she said and I let go of her leading her into the front room, the first girl I had taken in there since Alice all those years ago.

" I've got to make a quick phone call first." I told Jessie as she settled herself into one of the armchairs.

I returned to the hallway and dialled the number for the hospital, asking for Mum's ward. The nurse on duty said there was no change in Mums condition so I asked her to pass on my love to her and Dad and to tell them I would be there first thing in the morning.

" Can I have a glass of water?" Jessie called from the front room as I put the phone down.

Without replying I went into the kitchen and poured her a drink from the tap.

" Thanks," she said when I returned with the glass and she took a huge gulp from it, " I couldn't help but overhear," she continued after swallowing the mouthful of water, " is your Mum in hospital?"

" Yes," I answered, " she's not been too well lately."

It wasn't that I didn't want to tell Jessie about Mum it just didn't seem to be the right moment so I quickly changed the subject.

" So tell me about the car crash."

" It was last night," she began, " just after eleven all hell broke loose in our house. Dad went completely mental, smashing the house up and everything."

I could see that Jessie was starting to shake again so I moved over to where she was sitting to comfort her.

" He'd just taken a phone call from the police, his girlfriend had just died from injuries suffered in a car crash."

Jessie was starting to speak very slowly and I could see that she was about to start crying so I put my hand onto hers.

" Oh Jessie," I said, " I'm so sorry."

" Apparently she was on her way to see him and

asked the police to call him while the firemen were trying to cut her out. She died just before they could make the call."

" My God Jessie, that's so awful, your Dad must be devastated, shouldn't you be at home with him?"

" He's the reason I had to get out, he's so angry, me and my brother were so scared we had to get away."

" He's probably just hurting so bad, you should go and talk to him."

" I can't, he's always been aggressive, he takes it out on us, even more so since Mum died."

" Perhaps it's bringing back memories of that."

" You're not listening to me, if I go back home he'll probably hurt me, he can't control his anger and just hits out at anything that gets in his way."

" You can stay here the night if you want to."

I had hoped to be asking Jessie that question anyway but under different circumstances. I hadn't expected to be talking to her about anything like this but strangely I was finding out a lot more about her than I probably would have done if things had been normal. I felt extremely sorry for her as she seemed to have suffered a lot in her life. I wanted to hold her in my arms again and make her pain go away.

" I'd like that," she replied to my question

before continuing, " I'm sorry, I messed up your night. I was really looking forward to seeing you."

" That's o.k." I interrupted, " you can't help what's happened. I'm glad you turned up, I don't know what I'd have thought if you hadn't."

" Prick teaser, probably." Jessie laughed and it was good to see. I needed to keep that mood going, to take her mind off what had happened so I kept asking her questions about herself, what she had done with her life so far, what her ambitions were, the conventional things that people talk about on a first date. We talked for what seemed like hours making each other laugh and I felt we had more in common with each other than I had ever imagined possible. Even the bad things that Jessie had briefly mentioned when she first arrived seemed to be on a level with all the shit I went through in my younger years. Not the parental abuse though, I had never experienced that and could never understand how anyone could harm their children whatever the circumstances.

It was nearly three in the morning and I thought we were going to be up all night talking when Jessie said,

" Can we go to bed now?"

I stopped whatever it was I was talking about and just looked at her slightly shocked. She shocked me further still when she added, " Together."

CHAPTER TWENTY-SIX

Jessie was wrapped around my body when I awoke at about seven thirty. I looked down at her resting against my chest and felt her warm breath on my skin. She looked happy, at least happier than when I had brought her home. I hoped she wouldn't think that I had taken advantage of her but then remembered that it was her idea to sleep together. I recalled the nervousness I felt as I led her to my room and got beneath the sheets with her. She was scared and even though I wanted her badly I told her she didn't have to if she didn't want to.

" It's my first time," she said and I could almost hear her heart beating out of control. I remembered my first time with Alice and when I looked at Jessie it was as though Alice was still there with me. I hadn't noticed before but there were a lot of similarities in the way she looked and the way I still remembered Alice.

I was as gentle as I could be and Jessie fell asleep in my arms afterwards. We had spent just a few hours together and already I was falling in love with her in a big way.

Trying hard not to disturb her sleep I eased her off me and got out of bed. She stirred and reached out her arm as if to find me but didn't wake. I dressed quickly and went downstairs.

I had to call the hospital first to check on Mum and as I put the phone down afterwards I heard footsteps behind me. Turning round I saw Jessie coming down the last few stairs dressed in one of my t-shirts.

" I heard you talking." She sounded very tired and let out a yawn as she crossed the hallway and put her arms around me pulling me close to her body.

" You should have stayed in bed a little longer." I told her after we had shared a passionate kiss.

" I wanted to be with you."

She spoke in a slightly childish voice and fluttered her eyes at me. I wanted her again right there in the hallway but I broke away from her and walked off in the direction of the kitchen.

" I've got to go to the hospital," I called out to her, " what are you going to do? You're quite welcome to come with me if you want but there's something you should know first."

" What's that?" Jessie asked as she came up behind me putting her arms around my waist. I wasn't used to the attention I was being given but it was something I had craved for a long time. I found it difficult to concentrate as she kissed the back of my neck and I span around in her arms to kiss her full on the lips. It was all too much for me; I had to make love with her again. I tried to guide her towards the stairs but we never made it instead satisfying our mutual lust on the kitchen floor.

I lay in her arms afterwards listening to her laboured breathing until she started to shiver. I looked around and retrieved her discarded t-shirt handing it back to her with a smile.

" You're so beautiful." I said casting a look over her trim body. Jessie blushed and turned her head away clutching the shirt to her breasts as though she didn't want me to see them. Getting up she left the kitchen to go upstairs and I watched her naked bottom until it disappeared from view.

I'd made us both a mug of coffee by the time she returned fully clothed and she sat next to me at the kitchen table as we drank.

" What did you want to tell me?" Jessie asked.

I took hold of one of her hands and looked directly into her eyes.

" It's about Mum," I began, " she's dying of cancer and she's probably only got a few hours to live."

Jessie looked stunned.

" I want to show you something." I continued,

getting up and disappearing into the front room. I came back holding in my hand a black and white photograph.

" This is Mum," I said handing the picture to Jessie, " if you come with me to hospital then this is the person you will be looking at not the one that's lying there."

" Don't!" Jessie looked up at me, " that's so sad, you'll have me crying in a minute."

" I'd like you to come but I'll understand if you don't, you've got things in your own life that need sorting."

" I can do that later, I'd like to meet your Mum because you'll never meet mine." Jessie sounded really sad when she mentioned her own mother and I could tell that she missed her badly.

" You'll have to tell me about her one day."

" I didn't really know her, she died when I was very young," she replied with more than a hint of bad feeling and then changing the subject completely said, " shall we go?"

Her sadness had almost changed to bitterness by the way she spoke and I could tell there was something about her mother's death that bothered her, I hoped she wasn't blaming her mother for dying.

We caught the bus in to see Mum and Jessie didn't stop asking questions about her, what she was like, how she had brought me up, the things we had done together and I was a bit concerned. I got the impression that Jessie was searching for something but when I tried to talk about her own upbringing she became evasive, especially if I mentioned her own mother. She was hiding something and I needed to find out what it was.

As it happened Jessie didn't stay long at the hospital, she took one look at Mum and I could tell by her eyes that she was unhappy about being there. I thought maybe that it was something to do with her Dad's girlfriend dying and that she had finally realised that she should be at home with him. Tearfully she said sorry to me but that she had to go and be on her own for a while. I scribbled my phone number on a scrap of paper and told her to call me and to keep on trying if I didn't answer. We hugged each other tight and parted with a kiss. I watched from the window behind Mum's bed until I saw her walk across the car park and out of the hospital grounds towards the bus stop. I hoped she would be alright.

Dad mumbled his approval of Jessie as I turned my attention back to my parents but he thought that she was a little on the young side.

" I hope you know what you are doing," he said. Jokingly I replied that I was too old for fatherly advice but Dad just shrugged his shoulders.

Changing the subject he asked if I had managed to find Mulvey but I had to say that I hadn't and that I needed to go and phone around again. I'd remembered to bring the numbers I had for his flat and the club and I went downstairs to call from the hospital payphone. I tried his flat first and was somewhat relieved when I heard his voice on the other end of the line.

" Thank God," I said, " are you alright?"

It was a stupid question really as somehow I knew he wouldn't be. He sounded a lot calmer than he had been the other day but there was still a nervous edge to his voice.

" I need to talk to you Roo, urgently."

" O.K but you'll have to come to me," I told him, " I'm not leaving Mum."

I explained everything about the past couple of nights with Mum and how she was clinging to life and he agreed to meet me at the hospital café an hour later. I said goodbye and checked my watch, it was just on eleven o'clock. Good, I thought, I can have lunch at the same time as talking to Mulvey and not be away from Mum too long.

Mulvey turned up late and didn't look good. He peered anxiously around the seating area of the café before finally catching sight of me. Hurriedly he came over and sat down opposite. I asked if he would like a drink and he readily accepted my offer thrusting his hand into his pocket to pull out a fistful of coins.

" Help yourself," he said dropping the money onto the table and pushing it in my direction. I declined to accept his cash and went to fetch him his drink. When I returned I noticed that Mulvey was tearing a paper serviette into small pieces. I had never seen him in such a state and wondered what could have turned such a big confident man into the nervous wreck he now seemed to be.

" O.K so what happened with Sami?" I asked, referring to his planned meal and proposal of Thursday night.

" She's dead."

The words burst out of Mulveys mouth a lot louder than he intended and he looked around the room to see if anyone had noticed before saying it again, this time in a whisper.

" She's dead Roo."

I automatically assumed he was trying to tell me that he had done it, that he had killed her.

" Oh my God Nick," I kept my voice down to a barely audible whisper, " what have you done?"

He shot me an angry look and I regretted my assumption immediately as he spoke.

" Nothing," he said still glaring at me, " there was a car crash."

His words shook me rigid, not another one I

thought. I pictured Jessie telling me the same thing the night before. What was going on? Then I remembered the hospital receptionist telling me there had been two car accidents on Thursday night when I had been trying unsuccessfully to contact Mulvey.

" I'm so sorry Nick, what can I say, you...you were going to ask her to marry you."

" I did, it all went wrong."

What did he mean? Surely if she had died in an accident he wouldn't have had the chance to ask her.

" I don't understand?" I said hoping for an explanation.

" She turned me down, it was so perfect, the meal, the flowers, the candles... I thought I'd done everything right and then I get the ring..."

I could feel his emotion, the pain he was going through was so real that I was sharing it with him.

" ...I asked her to marry me and she turned me down. It was awful Roo. She was the love of my life and she said no. I asked her why but she just said she had to go, I tried to stop her, I couldn't just let her walk out on me. She told me that it was over, that she loved someone else. I chased after her but she locked herself in her car, she wouldn't talk to me and drove off. I followed in my car, we were driving too fast... she lost control and hit a wall, I panicked and carried on driving."

" You didn't stop to help?"

" I couldn't, I was scared. I drove back a little later and there were people everywhere, ambulance, police and fire brigade trying to cut her out. I came back home and tried to call you, you weren't in."

Something Mulvey said had got me thinking, it was too similar to what Jessie had told me, Sami being cut out by the firemen. He also said there was someone else, surely it was too much of a coincidence that Sami was Jessie's Dad's girlfriend. I had to ask Jessie her name and I certainly couldn't tell Mulvey what I was thinking. I had to make sure I had got it wrong about Sami before I could help him. I told him he had best go home and shut himself away from everything for a few days but he said he couldn't because of the club, he needed to be there. I managed to convince him that I could hold the reins for a while and arranged to meet him at four before the club opened so he could give me the keys. We parted company with a hug and I told him everything would work out alright in the end, then I went back to Mum's ward to break the news to Dad and tell him that I had to leave once again.

CHAPTER TWENTY-SEVEN.

" I've decided to go away for a few days,"
Mulvey informed me as he showed me around the
club office letting me know the combination of the
safe, " John knows everything about running
things and I trust him but I feel more secure
knowing you'll be here too. I can't thank you
enough for this."

" Save it," I said, " you just go and get your
head straight and we'll deal with everything else
when you get back."

" You're a good friend Roo." Mulvey declared as
he continued to show me all that he thought I
needed to know. Finally he was satisfied he had
told me enough and we left the club together.

" Goodbye," I said as he handed me the bunch
of keys I had come to collect, " take care."

I caught the bus back home as I didn't fancy
taking a taxi. I wasn't in the mood for idle chitchat
with a nosey cab driver. I needed to take time out
to think over a few things and felt the bus journey
would help me to do that. My main thoughts were
of Jessie as I gazed out through the window, I
needed to talk to her as soon as possible especially

after what I'd heard from Mulvey earlier. I was becoming more and more convinced that Sami was the person her Dad had been seeing but I needed her confirmation. Whatever she told me there was no way that I could tell Mulvey what Jessie's relationship with Sami was. I couldn't even remember if I had told him I was seeing Jessie and if there was any truth in what I believed and Mulvey found out I hoped he wouldn't take any of it out on her. Even though it was Sami who was to blame she was dead and he would probably need a scapegoat to satisfy his anger, I just prayed it wouldn't be my innocent Jessie.

I'd only been in the house for about two minutes when the phone rang and to my delight it was Jessie. She told me she was missing me so much that she'd been calling me every five minutes hoping that eventually I'd be at home. She sounded so happy that although I desperately needed to ask about her Dads girlfriends name I felt I couldn't do it over the phone, I needed to be with her when I asked just in case it upset her too much. I told her I was looking after Mulvey's club for a few days while he was away but didn't tell her the reason why he was going. She asked if she could meet me there around six o'clock and I said that would be wonderful but unless she put the phone down soon I wouldn't be there until seven. She let out a laugh, blew loads of kisses at me and put the receiver down without saying goodbye.

With the dialling tone still ringing in my ears I looked at my watch, it was five fifteen, not enough time for the bath I'd planned and only just enough time to get changed into something suitable for running a club. I called for a cab and dashed upstairs to get ready. Ten minutes later I was fastening my shoes when the taxi's horn sounded outside. I felt good and couldn't wait to see Jessie. The barman, John, wasn't coming in until seven thirty and it was up to me to get things ready before the club opened, normally at eight on a Saturday night. I was glad that Jessie had said she was coming in because I was a bit apprehensive about setting things up even though John and the other staff would sort out anything I forgot when they arrived.

I unlocked the outside door and flicked on every light switch I could find before climbing the stairs and opening the doors to the bar and dance floor. The banging on the front door made me momentarily jump before I realised that it was probably Jessie trying to get my attention to let her in. I made my way downstairs again to open the front door and we embraced when we saw each other sharing a long passionate kiss. She looked gorgeous and when I told her so she gave me a playful punch. I picked her up and carried her over my shoulder up the stairs smacking her backside as I went, only stopping when we reached the dance floor where I set her down and crazily over mimed a slow dance with her. She giggled all the way through it even though I kept telling her to be serious.

" Idiot!" she laughed when it was all over.

" You know me so well." I replied as deadpan as I could before falling into fits of laughter. I could see our relationship being non-stop fun and I couldn't wait to take her out properly but as much as I wanted to continue acting the fool I had work to do.

" Give me a hand," I said, picking up a pile of bar towels and throwing them towards her, she dropped the lot, " and when you've finished picking those up you can put the ashtrays out."

I ducked as a couple of rolled up towels came back through the air towards me.

We set up everything as best we could and I took the floats out for both of the tills behind the bar. I checked the levels of the optic bottles and although one or two of them were getting low I decided that was John's domain and he could do it when he arrived.

It was seven o'clock when we'd finished; we had a

spare half hour so I sat Jessie down at a table with a drink. It was time for me to ask her.

" Can I ask you something?" I said to her as we held hands across the table.

" Do I have to answer?"

" Not if you don't want to."

" That's o.k. then."

" Your Dad's girlfriend," I began, " what was her name?"

" Samantha, Sami," she replied, " why?"

I suddenly realised that I hadn't thought of a reason why I wanted to know.

" Err... just curious about your life I guess." I tried to sound as convincing as possible and threw in another question to try and coax more information out of her.

" How well did you know her?"

" Not that well, we had only met a couple of times. I thought she was a bit of a tart."

" She wasn't like a step mum then?"

" No, I've never had a step mum, I never had a mum really, at least not one I knew."

Jessie sounded sad and I felt the conversation was going the wrong way, I wanted to talk about Sami but Jessie no longer did.

" It's what I've hated most about my life," she carried on before I had chance to speak, " Dad's endless succession of girlfriends, none of them lasting very long. They couldn't put up with his anger and eventually left him."

" It must have been really difficult for you not to have a mother to turn to then, you must really miss that."

Jessie gripped my hand really tightly and I saw a pained expression on her face, it reminded me of how she looked when she first told me about her mum dying and I knew she wanted to tell me something.

" If I tell you a secret will you promise that it will go no further?"

" Of course it won't." I replied, I had enough secrets of my own hidden away to know that the least people knew about certain things the easier it was to get on with life.

" They said it was an accident but I know the truth, I saw it happen, I was three years old." Jessie spoke solemnly and took a huge gulp from the drink I had given her.

" I saw Dad kill Mum and I didn't tell anyone about it."

It was my turn to take a drink; I was so sickened by what I was hearing I had to, to take away the nausea.

" What happened?" I eventually managed to blurt out.

" I remember them arguing, they always did, I

was at the bottom of the stairs when I saw him push her. She landed at my feet... her body was all twisted..."

Jessie was crying as she recalled the story that she had kept concealed for so long and it took a lot of self-control for me to stop myself from joining in. I told Jessie that she didn't have to tell me any more if she didn't want to but she said she needed me to know everything.

" They, the police, thought Mum and I were alone in the house and that it was a terrible accident. Dad had arranged toys at the top of the stairs and upended a laundry basket of dirty clothes around where she fell to try and make it look convincing."

" Didn't they ask you what had happened?"

" They tried but I wouldn't speak to anybody, not a word to anyone for about six months, they put it down to the trauma of seeing Mum fall but they didn't know the real reason."

" Who found her?"

" Dad called for an ambulance about five hours later pretending he had just come home from work and they believed him"

" And he spent the rest of your childhood hurting you?"

" It was his way of keeping me in line so that I wouldn't tell anyone about it. I couldn't, I was so scared I thought he would kill me too."

I heard the outside door open and the sound of voices as John and other members of staff started to arrive. I didn't want anyone to see the state Jessie was in so I took her into Mulvey's office where she sat in his chair, her face buried in a handkerchief that I had given her. I told her that I would be back in a few minutes and left her alone whilst I went to talk to John.

Because of the work I had to do I knew I couldn't leave Jessie in the office all night and I thought she would feel uncomfortable sitting at the bar on her own so I offered her the opportunity to go and stay at my parents house. I was surprised when she turned me down saying she had to go home. After what she had told me I thought that would be the last place she wanted to go but she said that for the first time ever she actually felt that she could deal with her Dad. I was worried about her safety and I made her promise before she left that if she ever felt threatened again then she had to come and find me.

CHAPTER TWENTY-EIGHT

With Jessie gone I returned to helping John at the bar. The doors had opened and the first few customers had drifted in. The D.J. had arrived late and was still busy setting up the sound system which was beginning to worry me a little. John said not to as it wasn't often he was on time on a Saturday night and anyway Mulvey never minded because he was the best D.J. around.

I soon got into the swing of things behind the bar, the prices were a bit of a problem to start with but none of the customers complained. Everyone seemed to be in a great mood and one or two recognised me from my recent performance on stage. I had quite a few requests to dance during the evening but my mind was too focused on Jessie to say yes to them. I hoped she had got home safely and her Dad hadn't started anything with her. When everything was all over and I felt confident my Dad would be able to cope on his own I decided I was going to ask Jessie to come back with me to my own house where I could take care of her all the time. It would be a new start for both of us.

The night was passing by very quickly thanks mainly to the drinking habits of the club's clientele. I had never seen so many people drink so much in such a short space of time. I thought I could drink a lot but I was nothing compared to those I was serving. I didn't know how Mulvey could do a job like this, I was shattered after just four hours.

The frantic atmosphere of the club seemed to ease as it passed midnight and I took a walk from behind the bar to collect some dirty glasses. I was cleaning a few tables near the back wall when I noticed someone I recognised sitting alone. Mary was clutching a glass but I didn't remember serving her so I assumed one of the other bar staff had done so. I hadn't forgotten our chat the other night when she had left the café so abruptly and I was just about to go and say hello when she got up and moved to sit in a chair next to the one she got out of. I thought it a bit strange so I just watched her for a while. She seemed to be looking at something. I followed her gaze and noticed she was staring at two youths who were sat chatting at a table not too far away. I wondered what could be the attraction of them; I didn't think Mary was the type to be picking up young boys at night. I thought I recognised one of them as one of the group I had bought drinks for the first time I had met Jessie. As I watched they both stood up and finished their drinks putting the glasses down on the table before starting to walk towards the exit. I looked back at Mary and saw that she was fastening her coat so I moved quickly as if to clear her table while she was still sat down.

" Hello," I said in mock surprise, " I haven't seen you in here before, how are you?"
Mary tried to look around me but I was stood in such a way that it was impossible for her.

" I'm fine," she said but she sounded disappointed, probably because she had lost sight of the two boys, " I fancied a drink after work so I came in here."
I could tell she was lying so I took a chance and asked her if she wanted another. I expected her to say no but to my surprise she readily agreed.

" I'm glad I bumped into you," she said as I returned with her drink and one for myself, " I wanted to apologise for the other night."

" That's o.k. but what was it all about? We started talking about secrets and you just ran away."

" I know, I'm really sorry, it was something I haven't been able to deal with no matter how I look on the outside."

" Sounds serious, do you want to talk about it?"
I made the offer to listen to her but hoped she

would turn me down, I didn't think I could cope with any more problems that night.

" How long have you got?" Mary hinted that she did want to talk but I didn't feel up to it so I tried to change the subject.

" Who were those two youths you were watching?" I asked.

" They are part of the problem," she answered and I knew I was in for another long night, " I was following them, that is until you got in the way. I was hoping they would lead me somewhere, back into the past."

She sounded quite hurt and suddenly I felt sorry that I hadn't wanted to talk. I thought back to the time in the café and remembered that she had seemed terrified then. If she wanted to exorcise a few ghosts then I was going to listen to her.

" Why would you want to go back to the past?" I asked.

" So that I can stop the future from being totally fucked up."

" I think you had better explain."

" One of those lads was my son and the other is..."

She stopped talking mid sentence and shut her eyes tight.

" Shit," she said after a few moments, " I can't do this."

" No one can help you unless you do."

" Maybe I don't need help, maybe I can sort this on my own."

" But what if you can't?"

Mary gave a dejected sigh.

" I don't know, I really don't know."

She didn't say another word for the next ten minutes; she just sat there in her chair staring down into her lap. I didn't know what she was thinking but guessed it was probably whether to continue telling me just what it was that was troubling her so much. I fetched us another drink each and it wasn't until I put them down on the table that she noticed I had been to get them.

" Thanks," she said, " I've been thinking, you're right, I do need to tell someone. There's something I've never told anyone before in my life, not even my parents."

Her words struck a chord with me and I shuddered as I thought back to my sixteenth birthday. Nothing Mary could tell me was likely to shock me; I couldn't imagine anyone could have ever been through a worse experience than what had happened to me. Not even Jessie's confession that she had seen her Dad kill her Mum compared to my horror.

" It happened sixteen years ago," Mary continued, restoring my attention back towards her, " I'd managed to put it all behind me and get on with my life until last week. I blame myself, if Mikey had a Dad then none of this would be happening."

" Is Mikey your son?"

" Yes and I love him no matter what."

" Is he in some sort of trouble?" I was getting a little confused; I thought Mary's problem was in her own life not her son's.

" I'm not sure, that's what I need to find out, please let me finish."

Mary was adamant that I didn't interrupt until she had told me everything so I sat back and listened.

" Like I was saying, I blame myself...Mikey's gay... he told me about it three months ago, I've been to hell and back over it, there has only been me in his life and I've been too overprotective of him. He never had the rough and tumble a boy should have, the side of life only a father can give."

I broke my silence, Mary was torturing herself unnecessarily.

" That doesn't mean he wouldn't have turned out gay, it's not your fault."

" I'll always blame myself... anyway I accepted it, I had to or I would have lost him that is until last week when I met his boyfriend for the first time. That's when it became real. That's when it became wrong."

Mary was still talking in riddles and it wasn't making any sense to me. What had Mikey's boyfriend got to do with her past?

" Mikey introduced Dean to me last weekend and told me they were a couple. There was something I recognised about him. He was the spitting image of Mikey's father."

Mary started crying and I had to get her out of the club before people started staring at us. I put my arm around her and told her to come with me into Mulvey's office where we could be alone. I hadn't noticed the time and was a bit surprised to find John in there counting the money from one of the bar tills. I asked him if he could leave us alone for a while.

" Sure." he said taking one look at Mary. She sat down in the chair vacated by John and wiped the tears from her eyes.

" So who was Mikey's father? Did you part on bad terms? Is that why you're ... I don't know... is that why you're wary of Dean?"

It seemed to me that Mikey's relationship with Dean was what Mary couldn't deal with, not the fact that Mikey was gay. Mary must suspect that Dean was... oh my God! I'd just realised... if Dean was the son of Mikey's Dad then he would also be

Mikey's brother. Shit, no wonder she was in such a state. Mary looked at me and she knew from my reaction that I'd worked it all out. Her tears started flowing as she spoke.

" There's more," she said, " I was fourteen... he raped me!"

I looked at her in stunned silence. Whatever it was I was expecting her to tell me next it certainly wasn't that. I had to get her out of the club, I had to help her and we needed somewhere to talk privately. If her fears were true then something had to be done quickly. Taking her back to Mum and Dads house was the only option I had.

John knocked on the door while I was thinking, he was carrying the draw to the other till. Everything had been done and everyone else had gone home he informed me so I told him to go as well and that I would deal with the money and the locking up. I took the takings from him and put them straight into the safe along with the other till draw and then locked it.

" You're coming back to my place, no arguments." I told Mary as I picked up the phone and called a cab.

I poured Mary a drink of scotch as she took her coat off and went into the front room. I'd grabbed the bottle from behind the bar as we'd left because I thought we both could use a drink considering what we had to talk about. We didn't discuss much in the taxi home, in fact Mary barely said a word. My mind was spinning; I was trying hard to piece together everything that Mary had told me so that I could talk logically once we got into the confines of the house. I needed to know everything including details of the rape no matter how hard it would be for Mary to talk about it. I contemplated telling her my own nightmare to make her open up to me but decided against it, it wouldn't have served any purpose least of all for me.

I took a swig of whisky from the bottle and put it back on the kitchen worktop and then taking a deep breath took both glasses into the front room.

" So tell me about the bastard who raped you."

I had to start somewhere and I thought it best to begin with the most painful part. If I could give her the impression that I hated him for what he had done to her then maybe she would find it easier to talk to me about it. Mary didn't answer and I thought maybe I'd been a little insensitive so I tried a softer approach.

" Did you know him?"

" No." Mary said quite firmly.

" How did it happen?"

It was a harsh question and I hoped Mary wouldn't think I was in any way going to blame her for what happened, I needed to get her to talk. She had to let me know everything she could remember about the man who raped her so that I could find out whether or not he was Dean's father.

" Did you know I was born in this town?" Mary asked me. I hadn't even thought about it and I wasn't given time to answer.

" I'm a local girl and as much as I love the place I've always had a dream to move away to try and forget, unfortunately circumstances have always stopped me, Mikey mainly. I have to walk past the spot it happened most days, do you know what that feels like?"

I wanted to shout back yes I know what rape feels like but this wasn't about me and anyway would she believe me if I told her. My pain was mine and I wasn't prepared to share it with anyone.

" I was fourteen when it happened and I will always remember it like it was yesterday. I was a happy little girl going home for tea after playing with my friends. It was only about a mile from where we are now when he grabbed me and dragged me into someone's garden. He smelt funny, I didn't know what it was then but now I know that it was alcohol. I can still smell it and I'm stupid enough to work in a pub. He talked to me as he did it, he wanted to know my name and I was so scared I told him it was Mary. He asked if I'd ever done it before but I didn't know what he meant so I said no. He laughed loud and said 'so you're a virgin Mary' and laughed again. I was crying with the pain but he didn't care and when he'd finished he picked up my pants that he'd ripped off me and just threw them in my face."

" And you didn't tell anyone?"

" You're the first and it's only because of Mikey that I'm telling you. I kept it secret, I was so ashamed. I thought it was my fault and then I found out I was pregnant. Mum and Dad were concerned that I wasn't eating yet I was putting on weight. They could tell by my shape that I was expecting a baby and took me to the doctors to make sure. It was a terrible time, too late to terminate. I still couldn't tell them I'd been raped so I lied to them that I'd been fooling around but I wouldn't tell them who with. They were angry but they stood by me."

" How old is Mikey?" I asked her.

" Almost sixteen, next month actually." she replied.

I was working things out in my head and realised that was about nine months after I had left home just after Alice had her baby, a baby she had named Dean. Surely they couldn't be the same people, no it was just too much of a coincidence. I started thinking about Jessie and how similar I had felt she looked to Alice. Jessie had said she had a brother and I had seen her and Dean together. I was starting to panic and I held my head in my hands saying 'oh my God' over and over again. Mary was really concerned.

" What's the matter?" she asked me.

" Do you remember the face of the man who attacked you?"

" Yes, I told you he looks like that lad that Mikey's been seeing."

" Can I show you something?" I said getting up and walking to the sideboard. I opened one of the cupboard doors and pulled out three cardboard boxes. They all contained photographs of me and my family when I was a child. I rifled through them quickly before finding what I was looking for. A photograph taken of the whole school the year before I left.

" Can you take a look at this."

I pointed to a figure standing in the back row.

" Is that him?"

Mary went white and she didn't have to answer, I knew I had found her rapist and I also knew I had found someone who hated him as much as I did.

CHAPTER TWENTY-NINE

I couldn't talk and neither could Mary. We both sat on the settee staring at the photograph that lay between us. I think we both would have sat there all night if we hadn't been disturbed by the phone ringing. My heart sank. I prayed that it wasn't the phone call I had been dreading, but it was, Mum had just died.

It was three o'clock in the morning and I needed to be with Dad, I also needed to be with Mary, I needed to talk to Jessie and I needed to be alone. I don't think I had ever cried as much before as I did that night and it was a good job that Mary was there with me. What had started out as me being there for her had turned full circle and we fell asleep in each other's arms.

We woke a few hours later on the settee still holding on to each other, everything that had happened was still fresh in my mind and I didn't know what to do first. Mary didn't know anything of what I was going through except the death of my mother. I had to get to Dad as soon as possible but I kept thinking that I had to contact Jessie first. I didn't know for definite that she was Tom and Alice's daughter but I was pretty sure she was. I couldn't phone her as I didn't know her number and even if I did what if it was Tom that answered. It would confirm everything but at the same time destroy my life completely. I felt sure that this was going to be unequivocally the worst day of my life. The more awake I became the more fucked up I was getting. I was asking myself too many questions and getting the answers I didn't want. I looked at Mary as she made me a coffee while I sat at the table in the kitchen and as much as I wanted to devote my attention to helping her I had issues of my own to sort out first and I needed to be alone.

" How well did you know him?" Mary asked me as she placed the cup of coffee down in front of me. I was a bit put out because I wasn't expecting her to start asking questions about Tom.

" Let's just say I know what a bastard he was and I hope for your sake that he isn't Dean's father."

" That's something I need to find out and soon."

" Leave it with me, give me your phone number and I'll call you but right now I need to be with Dad."

It was just the excuse I was looking for to be able to get rid of Mary and after finishing her drink she made me promise that I would sort it by the end of the day. I promised I would, I couldn't risk her going to find Tom herself because if he was Jessie's Dad then, knowing how aggressive he was, anything could happen.

" I'm glad I told you," Mary whispered in my ear as we shared a hug in the hallway, " I like you a lot."

Thankfully the phone began to ring and put an end to a potentially embarrassing situation. It hadn't even crossed my mind that Mary was thinking about me in such a way and I quickly said goodbye and picked up the phone.

" Hello." I said thinking that it must be Dad calling to ask when I would be coming in to hospital.

" Hi Roo, have you heard how your Mum is today?" came the response. It was Jessie.

" She's dead." I answered quite abruptly and as much as I didn't want to I carried on talking just as bluntly.

" What are your parent's names and is Dean your brother?"

" Look have I done something wrong?" Jessie questioned me.

" No, YOU haven't," I said trying to emphasise that whatever it was that I was upset about it wasn't her, " just tell me please."

" Well my Dad is Tom and my Mum's name was Alice and yes Dean is my brother. Why do you want to know?"

I couldn't give the real reason, not yet, but I'd thought of another one which would go a long way to explain my offish manner.

" You're fifteen aren't you?"

" Is that what all this is about?"

" I thought you were a lot older."

" Does it matter as long as we love each other?"

" Of course it does, I'm thirty three!"

" Roo, please don't do this, can I come and see you?"

Jessie sounded like she was beginning to cry and that was something I didn't want to hear. I hated myself for being so horrible to her but I shouted no and slammed the phone down. Now I was really fucked up. Jessie was Alice's daughter and that meant Alice was dead and Tom had killed her. I looked around the hall and caught sight of a reflection in the mirror. I didn't like what I saw, it seemed to be the image of Tom and he was laughing at me. I picked up a vase that was on the table next to the phone and hurled it smashing the mirror into a thousand pieces.

" You bastard." I screamed.

I didn't bother cleaning up the mess, I just left it as it was and made my way to hospital to meet up with Dad. He must have known that Alice was dead and I couldn't believe that neither he nor Mum had told me. They knew how much I liked her even if they didn't.

" Why didn't you tell me about Alice?" I shouted at Dad when I saw him. I didn't care that he was grieving for Mum; I was grieving too but over someone who had died years ago. At least he was with the love of his life when she died.

" We weren't talking and when we were I'd forgotten about it. You never mentioned her so we thought you had got over her. Please son I don't need this right now."

I was angry and I didn't want to talk to Dad let alone listen to what he had to say.

" Where's Mum?" I almost spat the words out.

" She's lying in the chapel of rest." Dad replied sadly. " Please don't be angry, we both loved you and wouldn't hurt you intentionally."

His words seemed hollow and I took no notice turning on my heels and marching off to where Mum lay.

The chapel was quiet when I entered and my angry mood dispelled when I saw Mum lying in her coffin. She looked even paler than she had done when I saw her last and her skin felt stone cold when I touched her face with my fingers. I kissed her gently on the cheek and told her how much I loved her. I wasn't even remotely religious but I sat down on one of the pews and said a prayer not only for Mum but also for Alice, Mary, Jessie, Mulvey and Dad. I knew I couldn't change the past but maybe I could do something to prevent the future being as bad. I had to make up with Dad first, no matter what his reasons were for not telling me about Alice I couldn't let it come between us. I couldn't let another life be destroyed.

I kissed Mum again and said goodbye closing the chapel door behind me as I left. Dad was waiting outside and he had someone with him. Jessie. She was holding a small bunch of flowers and she walked towards me when she saw me emerge through the door. She looked so like her mother and how I wished that she was.

" Can I put these next to your Mum please?" Jessie asked.

I looked into her wide pleading eyes and although I realised I couldn't see her again I knew I had to give her an explanation why.

" Yeah, be my guest." I replied almost nonchalantly, opening the door to the chapel again so that she could go inside. Jessie hesitated as if waiting for me to go with her but I told her I needed a word with Dad in private. I waited until the door had closed and then spoke.

" I'm sorry Dad, I had a really bad day yesterday, nothing but bad news that I found difficult to deal with."

" Do you think I had an easy night? Just go away son and come back when you're not being so fucking selfish."

Dad was normally a forgiving person and this was totally out of character for him, I had never heard him swear like that before, his words were sharp and hurtful. I had expected instant exoneration for what I had said to him but he didn't give it to me. He left me standing there virtually open mouthed in astonishment and went to join Jessie in the chapel.

I couldn't follow him in there, it just wasn't the place to have a heated discussion, so I waited outside. After a couple of minutes Jessie appeared.

" Your Dad says he's not coming out until you've gone. What happened? I thought you two were really close."

" It's got fuck all to do with you so why don't you just leave me alone." I yelled at her running towards a row of plastic chairs lined up against the wall and kicking out at one of them with all my might sending it crashing down the hallway. It was everything that Jessie didn't want to see, I was someone she cared about and I was being as aggressive and violent as her Dad. I lashed out again at another of the chairs but this time lost my footing and collapsed in a heap on the floor. I was getting out of control and I reached up grabbing the legs of the chair and throwing it hard into the opposite wall before turning and beating the wooden floor with my fists.

I carried on for a while until I felt Jessie's hands on mine trying as best she could to restrain me. I didn't want to hurt her so I gave in and just lay there, my heart beating rapidly as Jessie sought to calm me down.

" What is it Roo?" she asked, " It's more than just me and your Mum isn't it? Talk to me... please. I don't understand."

" You're too young to understand." I told her through my tears.

" Please... I deserve to know." Jessie begged trying to pull me up to face her.

" You're fifteen, the same age your mother was."

I wasn't making any sense to Jessie.

" What do you mean?" she asked.

" I was in love with her."

" You knew my mother?"

I stood up and wiped my eyes with the back of my hand.

" I'm sorry Jessie but I've got to go, I've got to

sort it."
I left her sitting on the floor, I could hear her calling after me but I didn't look around. If she followed then I didn't notice I just kept on walking until I was far away from the hospital.

CHAPTER THIRTY

All the time I was walking I was getting more and more wound up about everything. All I could think of was how my life had been a complete mess. I began to wish I had gone ahead and killed myself and then all the pain would no longer exist. I had no one but myself to talk to and I wasn't the best person to sort out my own problems. How I needed Jessie not to be Alice's daughter then maybe I could have someone to listen to me.

I kept imagining that Jessie could have been my daughter if Alice had chosen me instead of Tom and the image of having sex with Jessie was becoming abhorrent. I felt I had been screwing my own flesh and blood and it made me physically sick. The rush of vomit hit my throat at speed and I could do nothing to hold it back. I felt the eyes of everyone around staring at me as I threw up on the pavement. Bent double with my hands on my thighs I stayed there until the flow of sick had rescinded. I had to do something to alleviate all of my suffering. I had to put a stop to all the pain.

I stood up straight and looked around, there were still a few people staring and making what I presumed were unsavoury comments. I spied a phone box on the opposite side of the road. Reaching into the pocket of my trousers I pulled out a crumpled piece of paper with Mary's phone number on it. I needed to call her but I didn't know what the hell I was going to say.

I walked across the road and into the phone box grabbing a few coins from my pocket and putting them into the coin slot. Mary answered almost on the first ring.

" It's me Roo." I said in reply to her nervous hello.

" How are you?"

I knew Mary was genuinely concerned and I also knew that her pain was at least as great as mine so I felt a real affinity with her.

" I'm cracking up Mary," I answered, " but I had to call you. You need to know."

" It's all true isn't it?"

" Yes," I said, " Dean is Mikey's half brother."

" What am I going to do?"

Mary wasn't questioning me she was questioning herself and she kept on repeating it over and over again. I wasn't going to be any help to her so I just put the phone down and left.

The mental picture of Thomas James kept flashing into my mind as I walked in the direction of home. I was going to walk all the way as I didn't want to be around other people. In my mood I wouldn't be able to trust myself if anyone said the wrong thing to me.

The smug arrogant face of Tom was with me all the time and the force of every step I took was accompanied by the intense feeling that I was stamping it into the ground. He had brought so much misery to so many peoples lives that my hatred for him was fast becoming an obsession.

He had caused so much grief for me as I grew up, culminating in the brutality of my sixteenth birthday and got away with it. He had beaten and forced Alice into sex on her sixteenth birthday and got away with it. He had taken the beautiful Alice away from me and eventually killed her and got away with it. He had raped an innocent girl just fourteen years old and got away with it. He had been continually cruel and abusive to Jessie and Dean as they grew up and got away with it. He had even taken Sami away from Mulvey. How many other lives had he destroyed that I didn't know about. Mikey was about to be next when he found out that Dean was his half brother and that his father was his mother's rapist as well as a violent wife beating murderer. How was he going to cope with that, he'd probably painted his own image that the Dad he'd often dreamed about meeting was a wonderful person. Whatever I thought about protecting him for Mary's sake didn't matter; he had to know the truth.

I was almost home and I thrust my hand into my pocket to find the door key but instead brought out the bunch for Mulvey's club. All of a sudden I knew what I had to do. Once inside I made another call to Mary, she was still distraught about the situation and how to put a stop to it.

" Don't worry," I told her, " it will soon be all over."

" How?" she wanted to know but I didn't feel as though I could tell her.

" Is Mikey there?" I asked without answering her question. She said he was and I asked if I could have a word. Mary shouted to him to come to the phone.

" Hello," he said when he finally picked up the receiver.

" Hi Mikey," I said as friendly as I possibly could, I didn't want to make him defensive as I had never spoken to him before, " whatever I tell you now," I continued, this time a little more firmly, " I want you to keep secret from your Mum, do you promise?"

" It depends what it is." Mikey replied a little hesitantly.

" Can your Mum hear you?"

" I don't think so, she's gone upstairs, why?"

" I need you to come to Mulvey's club this afternoon and I need you to bring Dean with you."

" Why?" Mikey asked, " I don't even know you."

" But I know who your father is."

" What?"

" I can't tell you over the phone, your Mum mustn't find out. Come to the club at four."

I put the phone down, he didn't have the chance to protest so I knew that he would definitely be there. Next I picked up the phone book to search for the number for Thomas James.

It was easy to find, he still lived at the house he had grown up in. I dialled the number and waited. A gruff voice answered and despite the deepness I recognised it as Tom's.

I didn't bother with any niceties I just told him straight.

" Be at Mulvey's club tonight at five thirty. I have evidence to prove that you murdered Alice."

I was shaking as I slammed the phone back into its cradle and out of the corner of my eye I glimpsed the half drunk bottle of scotch that I had been sharing with Mary. I unscrewed the top and poured the fluid down my throat. I was so used to the burning sensation it made I didn't stop until it had all gone. It took about ten minutes to take effect and it was like an adrenalin rush. I was on a high the like of which I'd never felt before; I was going to get back at that bastard once and for all.

CHAPTER THIRTY-ONE

I made it to the club at half past three, I had things I needed to do before Mikey and Dean arrived. I went into the office and tidied it up as quickly as I could. The desk was set at one end of the room with the safe in the corner behind it. At the other end there was a couch where Mulvey sat occasionally when meeting with new suppliers. He had told me once that he always preferred an informal approach to new business. He felt potential clients would be more relaxed and receptive to his terms rather than the other way round.

I wasn't going to tell Mikey that his father was coming to the club because I felt that would spoil the surprise I had lined up. I went back to the bar and took down a bottle of scotch from the shelf. I poured three glassfuls and carried them over to a table near to the office door then I went to sit at the top of the stairs to wait.

Mikey and Dean arrived right on time, I guessed Mikey was eager to hear what I knew about his Dad. There was just one problem with that, I was going to tell him the biggest pack of lies he had ever heard. I didn't even care; he was just going to be a pawn in my desire to get even with Tom. Whatever he thought afterwards wasn't my problem, we would all be free, Mary, Mikey and me.

I opened the door to let them in taking care to close it again behind me. I didn't want a manic Tom barging in before I was ready.

Mikey was keen to know who his Dad was before he had even got halfway up the stairs but I told him to be patient and all would be revealed. We went into the club and I ushered them over to the table I had prepared.

" A drink to the future." I said and raised my glass to them both.

" So what has your Mum told you about your Dad Mikey?" I asked him as we all sat down at the table.

" Nothing much really," he replied, " just that she didn't get to know him too well."

" I knew him very well, we grew up together."
At least that part wasn't a lie and I noticed the delight on Mikey's face.

" What was he like?"

" What do you think he was like?" I countered Mikey's question hoping that he would make it easier for me to lie to him.

" I don't know, Mum was always so evasive

when I tried to find out. I got the impression that he left her before he knew she was pregnant."

" You're right about that, he never knew about you."

I topped up both their glasses with the scotch but didn't add any to mine.

" Will I be able to meet him?" Mikey asked, giving Dean a quick glance and I noticed their hands moving towards each other's.

" If I can arrange it," I started to say, " ... maybe tomorrow."

Mikey let out a gasp and gave Dean an excited look before leaning towards him and giving him a hug.

" Hey, don't mind me." I said in mock embarrassment.

" Sorry, but I can't believe I'm going to meet him and Dean is my... erm..."

" It's o.k." I butted in, " I know, your mother told me. Another drink?"

I filled their glasses full and we chatted about Mikey's Dad and what he was going to say to him and what he wanted to hear back. Mikey and Dean edged closer together the more they had to drink and I knew it was almost time to take a gamble. I checked my watch, it was twenty past five.

" I'm not a prude or anything," I said to them both, " I know it must be difficult for you to spend time alone. If you want to go into the office there's a couch in there, you can... well you know."

They both looked at me in shock and then looked at each other and giggled. They had both drank so much they weren't going to turn the opportunity down.

" Well go on then." I almost barked the order and they both ran off still giggling. The door banged shut and I wandered off downstairs but not before taking a gulp of scotch from the bottle and the knife we used to slice up the lemons behind the bar. I wasn't sure how Tom was going to react when he arrived and needed to be ready just in case.

My pulse was racing as I slowly descended the stairs and I was only part of the way down when the knock almost frightened the life out of me.

" You!"

Tom recognised me the instant I opened the door to let him in and I took a couple of paces backwards to keep out of his way. My grip tightened around the handle of the knife I held in my jacket pocket.

" What's this all about?" he asked angrily.

" Tell me why you killed her?" I wasn't scared of him and I felt that somehow Alice was backing me up.

" I didn't, it was a fucking accident."

" No it wasn't, I can prove it, you pushed her down the stairs."

" You don't know anything." Tom said and started to move towards me.

" Jessie told me, she saw you." I gave a slight look up the stairs and Tom stopped in his tracks.

" Is that bitch here? She's just like her fucking mother. I'll teach her as well."

" So you did kill her?"

" Yeah, she told me about you, she was coming to find you. There was no way I was going to let her."

He pushed past me and started up the stairs.

" Where is she?" he snarled at me. I prayed that everything was going to plan.

" In the office." I said meekly and let him go, following a few paces behind.

I watched as he burst into the office to be confronted by the naked bodies of Mikey and Dean. Dean was facing the door and Mikey had his head down between Dean's legs.

" Dad." Dean shouted in surprise as his father stood there.

" You bastard." Tom yelled turning to face me. He didn't have a chance to move any further as I leapt forward and plunged the knife into his chest.

" Because of what you did to me I wanted this to be the last thing you ever saw. This is for everyone's life you ever fucked up. Mikey's your son too. The son of the girl you raped."

Tom fell backwards gasping for breath. I looked down at the blood seeping through his clothes and I looked at Mikey and Dean. I felt pity for them both. I turned and walked away. Somebody else could clean up the mess; I'd done my bit.

16-12-05

ISBN 141202931-7

9 781412 029315